Napoleon was no longer a threat

Waterloo was fast fading into memory and peace had come again to Europe. After long years of war, London was eager to return to uninhibited pleasure.

But not Harriet Yorke, whose mission led her to a world she had never known—a world of lush, spectacular town houses as well as hovels on dirty cobbled streets. A world of vast country estates and opulent warehouses filled with silks.

She was ready for all this, but there was one thing she hadn't bargained for: the darkly handsome Marquis of Capel!

Marguerite Bell
is also the author of
Harlequin Historical #3

A Rose for Danger

It was easy prey for a highwayman. The
carriage was a wreck. The reins had
been severed and all four horses had run
off. There were no houses in sight. The
fitful moonlight cast sinister shadows.

Then Juliet caught the sound of horses'
hooves. It could only be the dreaded
highwayman!

She should have been frightened but
she was strangely thrilled. Finally she
was to meet the gallant, romantic
horseman...and the fluttering of
her heart told her it would not
be the only meeting.

The Devil's Daughter

MARGUERITE BELL

Harlequin Books

TORONTO • LONDON • NEW YORK • AMSTERDAM • SYDNEY

Harlequin Historical edition published March 1978
ISBN 0-373-05008-9

Originally published in 1978
by Mills & Boon Limited

CHAPTER
ONE

ST. JAMES'S SQUARE, in the heart of the fashionable London of 1816, was enjoying a peaceful Sunday morning. All those good people who normally attended the various places of worship provided for them in the vicinity had already made their way to these edifices, and a beneficent calm hung over everything. There were no discordant sounds, like errand boys' voices or knife grinders' cries; no lavender sellers offering their wares or muffin men extolling the virtues of their delicacies to the accompaniment of tinkling little hand-bells. On the Sabbath day, at least, the "ton" – those delicately nurtured and somewhat rarefied human beings accustomed on other days of the week to parading for the benefit of their neighbours in all the trappings of their high station – were protected from all intrusive sounds and, wherever possible, sights, and remained for the most part within doors.

Certainly the occupants of the very impressive mansion belonging to the Marquis of Capel did not expect their Sunday calm to be shattered by such a rude sound as a hackney carriage drawing to a halt outside. The Marquis had retired to bed some considerable while after the first cock had started to crow, and was in no condition to be aroused even if the house was on fire.

In such an event his butler would have taken every proper step to protect him from the consequences of the outbreak whilst remaining discreetly on the outer side of his lordship's bedroom door. Any other course would have been unthinkable, certainly in the opinion of all those who knew the noble gentleman at all well, such as his housekeeper who had nursed him as a baby and later as a most determined toddler, and Pauncefoot, who had started life as a groom of the establishment and was now risen to be major-domo.

Unfortunately Miss Harriet Yorke, alighting from the hackney carriage with the assistance of the elderly coachman, had no idea at all of the kind of day-to-day régime that prevailed within the Marquis's household. She was in point of fact in a state of mild exuberance because she had at long last taken a most decisive step which she felt was almost certain to benefit before very long the charges she had left in the rural wilderness of Sussex. Why, even the Marquis's sister, the fashionable Lady Fanny, had said that there was no other course open to her but to "beard the monster in his den"!

And that was precisely what she was doing – or hoped to do.

She looked up at the front of the large town house and for the first time experienced a faint cooling of her spirits. The house was so very splendid, and, compared with Lady Fanny's cosy little establishment in Hill Street, of a kind of splendour calculated to put awe into the hearts of those rather far down the social ladder, such as the Harriet Yorkes of the world. Indeed, if she had had any proper idea of the complete insignificance of her position by comparison with that of the Marquis she would not have been arriving at his house at all – would not even have arrived in Hill Street.

She drew a deep breath. She was, after all, the daughter of a rear-admiral, and that was not such a very humble position, even if he had died penniless.

The coachman asked cheerfully if she wanted him to wait for her, and she looked at him with some surprise in her remarkably attractive clear green eyes.

"Why, no, I – as a matter of fact, I hadn't thought ... Well, yes, perhaps it would be better if you did wait. I shall not, I imagine, be a great while."

The coachman shrugged his shoulders indifferently.

"'Tis Sunday, miss. I'm not likely to be very busy today. I'll wait."

"Thank you." The smile with which she rewarded his willingness was like a sudden burst of sunshine on a peculiarly dull day, and the coachman was impressed by it. She might be wearing an extremely plain bonnet and a plainer pelisse, but when she smiled like that she was a positive beauty, and there was no doubt about it, she was a lady.

"Don't you worry, miss," he urged her with emphasis, "I won't budge an inch until you come out."

With another radiant smile directed exclusively at him she turned away and commenced the ascent of the short flight of steps before the front door. Pauncefoot had had the door open for a full five seconds before she reached it, having observed the arrival of the hackney carriage, and he found it nearly impossible to conceal his considerable astonishment as he looked down from his very superior height into the beaming, pastel-tinted face of this most unexpected morning caller.

"May I see Lord Capel, please?" Miss Yorke enquired with a brightness she hardly felt at the moment. "Will you please inform his lordship that I shall not detain him for long. Indeed, I will take up very little of his time, if he is at home. The name is Yorke – Miss Harriet Yorke."

The butler coughed, then placed one plump hand thoughtfully over his mouth and considered the position from all angles.

"You could tell him that it is in connection with his wards," Harriet added more urgently.

"His wards, miss?" Pauncefoot decided that this was something very new in his experience. Other young ladies had turned up at the house from time to time, desirous to see his lordship, but not one of them had thought of such an invention as this in order to gain access to the Capel residence and the noble ear of the present incumbent.

"Miss Verbena and Masters Robert and Ferdinand de Courcey," the caller imparted rather more breathlessly.

"I think perhaps you'd better come inside, miss," Paunce-foot said ponderously, after devoting another moment to somewhat disturbed reflection, and stood aside from the doorway to enable her to enter and be suitably impressed by the magnificence of the great entrance hall. He led the way to what was known as the small anteroom, saw her disposed on a fragile chair of gilt and satin, and then withdrew, presumably to acquaint his employer of what awaited him below stairs should he feel strong enough to face it. But in actual fact it was to the housekeeper's sitting-room that he directed his steps, and for a long time after that nothing appeared to move or stir in the house.

For the first ten minutes or so after being left to her own devices Miss Yorke scarcely realised that she had apparently been forgotten. The room was so delightful that it quite captivated her interest, and she left her chair to examine the various ornaments and the quality of the fluted silk lining the walls. The silk she decided was Venetian, and it was of a pale water-green colour which she found entrancing. The long curtains before the windows exactly matched it, and they were caught up into great swathes looped with golden cords to which giant tassels were attached. The mirror above the marble fireplace was undoubtedly Florentine, and she was much impressed by a china vase which she suspected had emerged from a certain famous factory in Dresden.

It was only when a grandfather clock at no great distance from her chimed the hour that the realisation smote her that she had been shut up for fully half an hour. She had no very detailed knowledge of the way servants should behave in an establishment such as this, but it did seem to her peculiar that she should have been left alone so long. Apart from the fact that her hackney coach was still waiting, it was rather inconvenient, since she had to return all the way to Paddington in time for a very early dinner with her friend Miss Marley, and she was growing a little tired of the enforced inactivity. Was the butler waiting for the return of his lordship from one or other of his clubs, which must be quite near by, or had his lordship bluntly refused to see her? In which case was the butler finding it embarrassing to impart such a piece of information to her? Particularly as it concerned three such important people as the Marquis's wards?

She had thought that the butler looked quite taken aback when she had mentioned their names, but it could have been her imagination.

She tiptoed to the door and opened it just a very little, but nothing was happening on the other side of the door. The marble columns soared to the ornate ceiling, and a Grecian figure upholding a flambeau at the foot of the grand staircase was as remote and uninterested as any Greek maiden long passed into oblivion might have been. A footman, in a very splendid livery, stood rigidly within a few feet of the front door and was obviously prepared to open it with alacrity should a vehicle more impressive than her hackney carriage approach the Marquis's residence.

She returned to her chair, which had proved not the most comfortable for a period of prolonged waiting, and sat in anticipation of someone remembering her existence for another ten minutes by the ormolu clock on the mantelpiece. During that time she thought she heard movements in the hall, a rustle as of a silk or bombazine gown, and a certain amount of whispering. Then the door opened a crack, and an eye was applied to the crack and concentrated all its attention upon her.

Miss Yorke began to feel quite outraged. She was about to

rise and protest – or, at least, demand some explanation – when the door closed again, very softly and cautiously. With every hair on her head – and each one of them of the fiery hue of a copper beech tree – bristling in indignation, she remained quiescent for another five minutes, and then was about to rise and fling open the door and depart from the house with the intention of informing her coachman that he must not wait any longer, when Pauncefoot himself appeared as if conjured up by magic and bowed very stiffly and apologetically before her. She noted that he averted his eyes as he addressed her following a somewhat awkward little cough.

"I'm very sorry, miss," he said, the cough apparently proving very troublesome, "but I'm bound to inform you as it isn't any use your waiting any longer."

"Oh!" Harriet exclaimed. There was a chilling coolness to her voice which brought a faintly perturbed look to his face. "But I'm sure you must be very well aware that I have already waited for at least an hour for someone to come and inform me of such a decision."

"Er, yes, miss ... I'm very sorry about that, miss," Pauncefoot repeated, striving after his most dignified and rebuffing manner. "But the truth is – the truth is his lordship – his lordship cannot, er – see you ..."

"He is, perhaps, not at home?" Harriet suggested.

The butler looked positively astonished.

"At this hour, miss?"

"You mean that he is not accustomed to early rising?"

"Well, not precisely that, miss – "

"Then he is indisposed?"

Pauncefoot positively brightened.

"Well, now, miss, you could, perhaps – you could perhaps say that – "

"In which case you conveyed my message to him, and said that it is absolutely *vital*, in the interests of three people who are dependent on him, that I see him some time today, since I am returning to Sussex tomorrow? You did make all this very clear to him?" Miss Yorke demanded, advancing a few steps until she was actually in a position to lay a hand on the butler's sleeve. The clear brilliance of her green eyes and the disconcerting directness of their gaze confused the ageing servitor in an unaccustomed way, and he looked round somewhat wildly in the direction of the door. "And yet you say his lordship absolutely *refuses* to see me – ?"

"I didn't say anything of the kind, miss." A dignified figure in black, with a chatelaine of keys dangling at her waist, stepped through the doorway, and Pauncefoot heaved a sigh of relief. "This is the housekeeper, miss. She'll tell you it ain't no manner o' use trying to see his lordship today, which being a Sunday he likes to be protected from anything in the nature of a disturbance, as you might say."

The housekeeper paused primly in front of Miss Yorke, regarding her with the cold grey eye which had already studied her with thoughtful care through the crack in the door, and echoed the sentiments of the butler with a good deal of emphasis.

"You could not have chosen a more unfortunate day to call upon Lord Capel, Miss Yorke," she said, in the polite but quelling tones she reserved for young females for whom no one had vouched, and who had the temerity to call unchaperoned upon a bachelor. "It is the one day in the week when he does not receive callers."

"But why not?" Harriet demanded, in astonishment. "Lady Fanny Bingham, Lord Capel's sister, whom I approached before I came here today, said that I might find it difficult to see her brother, but she did not mention his lordship's particular absorption with religion. In fact, very much to the contrary, she did actually state that he had other preoccupations ... And so much I had already heard on more than one occasion. So why cannot Lord Capel, if he is at home, see me on a Sunday when it is a matter of such very great importance?"

Once again Pauncefoot coughed, and he and the housekeeper exchanged a long look. That mention of Lady Fanny had disturbed them both, but the situation so far as they could see it was not greatly altered. The young lady had to be convinced.

"Perhaps you could make it convenient to call upon his lordship at some time during the next week – or within the next fortnight or three weeks, since there is every possibility that he will be paying a visit to Scotland within that time, and naturally we cannot be precise as to the exact moment of his return," the housekeeper suggested, jingling the keys at her waist. "Or could you not," she added, as if suddenly inspired, "*write* to his lordship?"

"I have already written him several letters," Harriet informed her, "but he has not answered one of them."

"Perhaps he did not receive them."

"Rubbish!" Harriet exclaimed, and turned away impatiently and started to pace up and down the room.

The two custodians of Lord Capel's Sunday peace and calm watched her with interest. She was so slightly and delicately made that there appeared to be very little of her, and yet the peculiar dominance and determination of her disposition were given away quite unmistakably by the slight prominence of her otherwise very shapely chin, and the flash in her green eyes when she sensed that she was about to be thwarted. Taken together with the violent red of her curls, and the manner in which she trod the Aubusson carpet as if it were of no greater value than a strip of perfectly ordinary and rather threadbare floor covering, Pauncefoot at least felt that the vague feeling of apprehension he sensed within his breast was not entirely irrational.

Indeed, he began to wonder whether he ought to have overcome his nervousness of his master, well-founded though it was, and made a greater effort to acquaint his lordship with the visitor's arrival.

Miss Yorke ceased disdaining the Aubusson carpet and drew on her gloves, smiling with unexpected sweetness. Indeed, the housekeeper found the quality of the smile so unusual and charming that she even attempted to smile back, in rather a wintry manner.

"Thank you, but I will not detain you any longer," Harriet said, moving towards the door. "I realise that I have chosen a most inappropriate time to call upon his lordship."

Halfway to the front door, and with the footman already in position to whisk it open for her and watch her departure with admiring eyes, she paused, and turning once more to Pauncefoot enquired:

"At what hour does his lordship normally dine?"

The butler was happy to be able to resume his customary dignity.

"Never before six o'clock in the evening, and sometimes even later," he had to admit. "He is inclined to look with very much disfavour on the habit some quite distinguished families have of dining between four and five o'clock in the afternoon."

"Obviously a gentleman of high fashion," Miss Yorke commented. "Inclined, no doubt, to despise the ways of his fathers. And on Sunday evening?"

"He will dine, without doubt, at his club," Pauncefoot answered immediately. "And afterwards he may visit another of his clubs, or simply walk home quietly and enjoy an early night."

"So the Sabbath does bestow some benefit on him after all," Harriet murmured, and keeping her head lowered so that the brim of her bonnet should conceal the sudden brightness in her eyes she fairly ran down the steps to her hackney carriage.

Her coachman was practically asleep on the box, but he

jumped down immediately he realised she was ready to depart.

"I shall require you this evening about seven o'clock," Harriet told him. "Are you quite sure you can be free?"

"Quite sure, miss," he responded, and thought how refreshing a quiet morning nap could prove to be. He felt as good as a new man, and stretched himself luxuriously.

CHAPTER
TWO

WITH the coming of dusk, a soft April dusk, and while Lord
Capel was setting forth from his mansion in St. James's
Square for his favourite club which, happening to be no more
than a stone's throw away, made it unnecessary for Pauncefoot
to summon a chair for him, Harriet Yorke, having dined at the
unfashionable hour of three o'clock at her friend Miss Marley's
house in Paddington, was also thinking about setting forth
and behaving in an extremely unorthodox manner.

All those people who thought of Miss Yorke as a demure
young woman, grateful for occupying a position which provided her with a roof over her head in addition to her bed and her
board, and fortunately for herself some congenial companion-
ship, should have remembered that her father, during his years in
the Navy, had acquired the sobriquet of Devil Yorke. On the
deck of his ship, whether at sea or in some far distant harbour,
he was monarch of all he surveyed, and put such a quality of
fear into the hearts of the stout-hearted sailormen who made
up his crew that he was often surprised himself by the curious
willingness on the part of more than one of them on several
separate occasions to offer up their own lives in order that his
might be spared. If he led them into the jaws of death they
made no bones about following. And ashore, a widower with
one small daughter who looked unbelievably like him, he constantly exhorted her to remember that God made Man,
Woman and the Devil, and the devil was the one to keep your
eye on. If you learned how to cope with the devil, and mis-

trusted his activities on all possible occasions, you might
acquire a little of the devil's wiliness yourself, but at least you
were never likely to be taken base advantage of. Other people
might mistake your endeavours, but so long as you were clear-
sighted enough you were never likely to go wrong.

Your conscience would be clear, and a clear conscience was
the next best thing to telling the devil to go to the devil!

Brought up in such a tradition, it was not surprising that
Harriet was seldom at a loss when beset by problems. Despite
his gallantry when afloat and determination when ashore,
Admiral Yorke had successfully dissipated two small fortunes
which had been left to him, and when his life was terminated
during a minor affray in the Aegean Sea he departed this
world without the comforting knowledge that his next of kin
would benefit in any way by his demise. In fact, she was left
penniless. Friends had rallied round, and one of them found
her the position of governess to Sir Willoughby de Courcey's
motherless daughter. Sir Willoughby had two sons, one who
went daily to conjugate Latin verbs at the local parsonage, and
another who was already at Oxford. Unfortunately, however,
from the point of view of both Harriet and the young de
Courceys, Sir Willoughby got himself thrown when out hun-
ting with local enthusiasts, and was brought home on a five-
barred gate. He died within a few hours, and when his will was
read it was discovered that he had made provision for his de-
pendents by appointing them wards of a certain very noble
gentleman, none other than the Marquis of Capel, heir to the
Duke of Coltsfoot, who had apparently accepted the obligation
without demur in addition to becoming treasurer of their
considerable family funds.

When weeks and then months passed following the death of
Sir Willoughby, and no indication was received from the Marquis that he intended to contact his wards or to shoulder his
new responsibilities, a certain anxiety began to permeate the

atmosphere at Lowthan Hall, where they resided. Naturally it was understood that Lord Capel was a very fashionable gentleman, with many claims upon his time and no doubt with a large number of friends who kept him preoccupied, but money was running short in Sussex. Little Mr. Moss, of Moss and Rutledge, the local firm of solicitors, said there was nothing at all they could do to alleviate the position without the consent of his lordship. They, too, had written to him, but without the smallest response. And Verbena was without a respectable gown to her name, Robert could not return to Oxford because there was no way in which his fees could be paid, and worse than that the cook was raising difficulties because the butcher refused to deliver the meat until his last bill was settled in full, and the local provider of groceries followed suit. There was a serious depreciation in the quality of the menus at Lowthan, two servants had already left to better themselves, and the head gardener had given notice – no doubt he, too, had decided that he could better himself.

There was no possibility that the butler would desert them, because no one else would employ him in his declining years. And the housekeeper, too, was loyal, and Penelope, the children's old nurse. But apart from that the situation was becoming intensely serious, and though she dismissed from her mind the thought of her own unpaid salary, Harriet sat down and indited her first letter to his lordship. It was followed by a second, and a third ... and there was absolutely no response.

A letter to Lady Fanny Bingham, the Marquis's sister, in Hill Street, brought an immediate response. She disclaimed all knowledge of any new obligations incurred by her brother, but suggested prompt action if anyone was prepared to take it; and as Harriet was the only one, apparently, who had thought it necessary to take rather more positive steps than the local solicitors, it seemed incumbent upon her to deliver her charges out of such a serious predicament. These were Lady Fanny's own words, and they gave Harriet the clear view that that lady was at least as realistic as she was herself.

So, taking heart from such an obvious challenge, and being more than certain in her own mind that her father would have acted long before, she drew upon her own modest resources and hired a chaise to take her to London. It was her first visit to the capital, and under normal circumstances she would have appreciated such an adventure to the full, but being constantly worried that her funds would not last out, and that Lady Fanny might refuse to see her, she finally arrived in Hill Street in a state of great trepidation.

But Lady Fanny did receive her, and Lady Fanny was hearteningly blunt.

"Beard the monster in his den," was her advice. "Don't waste another moment, but insist upon seeing him."

She was quite unlike anything Harriet had imagined, being the prettiest widow in her early forties anyone could possibly imagine, with a lively sense of humour, and clearly as much outraged by the position as anyone could desire. And if her sense of humour was rather more in the ascendant than her sense of outrage, then Harriet could not really complain. For Lady Fanny was extraordinarily gracious, offering to read her brother a lecture when she saw him next, and to point out to him the evils of such immoral conduct.

"For of course it is positively immoral to ignore those poor dear children," she said, with a spark of appreciation in her bright blue eyes that startled Harriet, who in any case could not quite see young Robert de Courcey in the role of a poor dear child. "Although why in the world he accepted such a charge in the beginning I cannot imagine. It is so altogether unlike him. He is entirely without love for children, and although I have racked my brains I simply cannot remember his ever having referred to this Sir Willoughby – whatever it is that you say his name is? Or, rather, was!"

"De Courcey," Harriet supplied. "I imagined they must be very close friends."

Lady Fanny shook her head.

"If that is so, then it is one secret he has kept from me. But of course I do not know all his friends."

She regarded Harriet a trifle more shrewdly, and enquired:

"You said something about a fortune . . . quite a considerable fortune, I believe you meant to imply? Is all this inherited by the young people you are here to represent?"

"It is divided equally among them," Harriet replied. "Sir Willoughby was particularly devoted to his youngest child, his daughter, and he saw no reason to make an unfair division."

"I see." The Marquis's sister tapped her cheek with a small ivory fan. "Well, I must say I am inclined to the view that your late employer was an extraordinarily enlightened man and one for whom I feel a growing admiration, since in so many families the girls are almost entirely overlooked, and this leaves the poor things with an abysmally low chance of contracting a suitable marriage. However, in this particular case we need not anticipate any such difficulty?"

"Verbena is scarcely eight years old," Miss Yorke told her a little drily.

"A pity," Lady Fanny commented. "I might have offered to bring her out next season, when I have undertaken to bring out a favourite niece of mine, if she had been just a little older. The youngest Montague child was only just turned fifteen when she married the Earl of Devenham."

She started to pace up and down her charming drawing-room, which was decorated almost entirely in yellow and was matched not only by the big bowl of daffodils in the window but by the delicate lemon kid slippers which peeped from beneath her lavender gauze gown. Harriet, though she knew

very little about high fashion, did not need to be told that Lady
Fanny Bingham's dress reflected her position as the daughter
of a duke who would receive a very generous portion under
the terms of her papa's will and who had been left a magnificent
fortune by the husband who had made her a widow at least
three years before. She obviously favoured the present mode,
and her robe was very slim and emphasised the delightful
outline of her extraordinarily youthful figure. In order to be
certain that her status as a widow was properly recognised
she wore a Flemish lace cap, trimmed with lavender satin
ribbons. Her curls, which were only partially looped up under
her cap, were so dark that by contrast with them her skin
seemed positively dazzling. And those vivid, kingfisher-blue
eyes of hers were fringed with eyelashes which a large number
of her friends insisted were darkened by the skilful fingers
of her maid.

"Well, well," she said, halting suddenly in front of Harriet
and smiling at her with a dazzling display of beautifully
even little teeth, "there is nothing more, I'm afraid, I can
do for you, Miss Yorke. But I do entreat you not to allow my
brother to continue to evade his responsibilities, and in all our
interests" – when thinking about it afterwards Harriet found
it difficult to decide in what way Lady Fanny's interests
could be served by anyone as obscure as herself – "in all our
interests you must continue most vigorously to champion
the cause of these de Courcey children. If necessary you will
have to camp out on the pavement outside my brother's
house in order to see him. Do not be put off by that ridiculous
Pauncefoot's efforts to protect him. And do not, above all,
lose heart if you do not see him immediately. Stick to your
guns, as my younger brother Bruce would say!"

She waved very pleasantly from the window as Harriet
descended the steps of the house rather thoughtfully, and
she succeeded in leaving an impression of a brightly plumaged

bird with the governess, but one to whom it might be a little unwise to approach too close. It might even be a little unwise to heed any advice she gave, but Harriet, after discussing the matter intensively with her own former governess, Miss Marley, realised that she had no alternative but to force her presence upon the Marquis. Having met his sister she decided that he had probably forgotten all about the obligations he had incurred when he promised the late Sir Willoughby that he would act the part of a father to his children. Lady Fanny would probably make a very charming mother when she remembered the existence of her offspring – if, indeed, she had any – but the smallest excuse to do something that excluded them would always be happily seized upon by her. Daughters would represent a problem because they had to be bestowed in marriage, but sons – well, sons could look after themselves. That was her attitude to her brother, whom she probably hardly ever saw; and if his attitude was exactly the same as her own . . .

And it obviously was.

Harriet, having paid one visit to St. James's Square that day, set forth again for a second visit with the determination not to be frustrated this time. At least Lady Fanny was right when she advised such a course of action.

CHAPTER
THREE

THIS time, very much to her relief, it was not Pauncefoot who opened the door to her. No doubt Pauncefoot, at that hour of the day, had other and better matters to occupy his attention, and it was the young footman who had let her out of the house following her morning visit who stood gaping at her in obvious astonishment and admiration when he answered her summons at the bell.

Harriet said immediately:

"I wish to see Lord Capel. If he is not at home I will come inside and wait," with a firmness she was actually far from feeling.

"I don't know about that, miss," the footman objected. "I mean, I don't know when his lordship –"

Harriet slipped past him into the candlelit hall. Despite the tall columns of wax in their glittering candelabra it remained shadowy, and to anyone who had no idea of the geography of the house it was somewhat confusing. To her all the solid mahogany doors looked exactly the same, and the corridor which led, she was sure, to Pauncefoot's pantry filled her with apprehension.

"The library," she said quickly, "I will wait in the library."

"But perhaps I'd better acquaint Mr. Pauncefoot –"

She turned and confronted him with such a commanding flash in her green eyes that he yielded immediately.

"Very good, miss."

When he had shown her into the library, and had seen the

way she cast an approving glance around it as if she were very knowledgeable about that kind of furnishing and architecture, and had no hesitation at all about seating herself in the most comfortable chair, he paused before closing the door upon her.

"Can I bring you some refreshment, miss?" he suggested. "A glass of Madeira and some biscuits –?"

"A glass of ratafia and a very few biscuits," she replied with a sweet, approving smile. "And there is absolutely no need to inform Mr. Pauncefoot that I am here."

She decided, when he had left her alone, that she was dealing with him in what her father would have described as a very low-down manner. It was more than possible that he would be taken seriously to task for admitting her to the house at all when such an item of intelligence did finally come to the knowledge of the Marquis's major-domo; and as for providing her with sustenance whilst she awaited the return of his lordship ... well, that would almost certainly be heavily frowned upon. She was reasonably certain that Pauncefoot had had his doubts about her from the moment she had descended from her hackney carriage that morning, and viewing the matter with detachment she could not but agree that her movements had a certain aura of suspiciousness about them.

But there was every possibility that Pauncefoot, in the absence of his master, and on a quiet Sunday evening, was securely closeted in his own particular sanctum, and he had probably already imbibed a sufficient quantity of his master's claret to render him rather more than indifferent to what was going on around him.

At any rate, Harriet hoped so. She very earnestly hoped that Pauncefoot would pass into a state of tranquil oblivion before the night had drawn to a close, she having no doubt that her vigil was likely to be a lengthy one.

By the time the delicate French clock on the mantelpiece had chimed the hour of nine, she had gratefully consumed the ratafia and biscuits. The library was particularly silent, at the rear of the house, and therefore with windows overlooking the garden. Occasionally Harriet tiptoed to one of the windows and looked out between parted curtains, but there was nothing at all to be seen. It was a moonless night, and she wondered whether Lord Capel would risk being attacked by footpads and walk back to St. James's Square from his club, once his evening there was ended, or whether he had arranged for his carriage to be driven to the club and return him to his house in greater comfort.

There were not many candles burning in their sconces, and finally several of them flickered, and one by one they went out. There was a fire burning in the grate, but that, too, merely smouldered.

She managed to stir one or two of the logs with her foot, and in the resulting, although purely temporary, bright yellow flame she was able to study the portrait which hung above the fireplace, and which she realised might very well be a portrait of the present Marquis's mother. She had a look of Lady Fanny, but the eyes were deep and dark and lustrous. Had the Marquis of Capel bright blue eyes, or did they resemble those of the lovely lady in the portrait?

Harriet sighed, and returned to her chair. She felt very much like an interloper, one whom the Marquis might very well order to be ejected from his house if he returned in the sort of mood that rendered his temper uncertain. Nevertheless, she wished that he would return, and that an end could be put to this intolerable situation.

It had never once occurred to her that when he did return he might be accompanied by one or other of his friends, or even that he might go straight upstairs to his own apartments. In the latter event, once the idea presented itself, she deter-

mined that she would have to inveigle him downstairs again.
Such an evening as this could not be altogether wasted.

But she was spared the ordeal of trespassing further into
the remoter recesses of this forbidding house when the Marquis
returned at ten o'clock. The little clock on the mantelpiece
had barely finished chiming the hour when she heard the
sound of voices in the hall. Unfortunately – and this she was
not prepared for – he was not alone.

Harriet sat upright in her chair, and then glanced round
wildly for some means of concealing herself – at any rate
temporarily. The voices were plainly male, and they were
approaching the library door with so little hesitation that she
had barely time to take the decision to rush to the nearest
window and seek the refuge offered by one of the long,
voluminous velvet curtains before the door itself opened.

Two gentlemen entered the library – what a relief, Harriet
thought, having discovered a peep-hole, that there were not
more of them, and that they both appeared to be reasonably
sober. In fact, they were completely sober. They were both
dressed in formal evening garments that were undoubtedly
the creations of first-class tailors, and the one who she
immediately decided must be the Marquis because of his
likeness to both the lady in the portrait and Lady Fanny Bingham had a scowl on his face that was the blackest she hoped
ever to see on the face of any man. Indeed, it even marred
the extraordinary symmetry of his features, and as his hair
was dark and his skin distinctly swarthy he reminded her
more of a very angry gypsy or a central European nobleman
than an English aristocrat.

He strode to the fireplace and kicked the logs into a blaze
with the toe of an elegant silver-buckled shoe, and then went
round resentfully seeking to infuse life into the guttering
candles. But despite his efforts the light in the library remained
poor.

His friend, who had seated himself in a chair by the fire, called upon him to come and sit down.

"We have enough to discuss, Rick, and very little time in which to do it," he remarked. "Why in the name of hell you should have embroiled yourself in such a manner as this I cannot think. We are all perfectly well aware that Aintree is a liar and a cheat, but there are others of our acquaintance who are not much better, and you have never thought it necessary to call them out. So why Aintree? And why now, when the situation is so devilish sticky about duelling?"

"If I kill him I can always go abroad," the Marquis said gloomily, staring down into the fire. "And as I almost certainly shall kill him you can kiss me goodbye after tonight, Charles – at any rate for a couple of years."

"Poppycock!" Charles returned. "You must be mad, man! The fellow is hardly known to you . . ."

"But his remarks were offensive," Lord Capel said broodingly, still standing in the middle of the rug before the fire and staring down into the flickering blue flames. "Deliberately so! And they concerned a – an acquaintance of mine . . ."

"A woman!" Charles exclaimed contemptuously. "Not even a lady!"

"And how would you define the difference between the two?" the Marquis enquired, as if he was genuinely interested. He looked thoughtfully at his friend, who was an attractive rather than handsome young man wearing a cravat that had been nothing short of a miracle of achievement when it left the hands of his valet earlier in the evening, but was a little crumpled and askew after an hour or so in one of his favourite haunts. "In my experience there is none. They both make demands – and they are both equally undependable!"

"Then in that case why are you risking so much in defence of one of 'em?" Charles reasonably wanted to know.

The Marquis of Capel shrugged his splendid shoulders, covered in a coat of dark blue velvet. His white satin small clothes and white silk stockings gleamed palely like the wings of a moth through the gloom of the library, and watching him through her peep-hole Harriet was temporarily diverted by the novelty of observing him. She preferred the looks of the young man seated in the chair by the fire, but the Marquis was something completely new in her experience.

"Six months in some hideout in Paris, and the rest of the time spent rediscovering Europe? What is so very terrible about that?" he asked. "I have many friends on the Continent. I shall enjoy looking to them for hospitality. It will be some small return for the many occasions when I have entertained them at Capel."

"But what of your family? Your father!"

"My father will be upset, of course, but the rest of my family will be merely diverted."

"The Duke will be more than upset," Charles Cavendish gave it as his considered opinion. He stood up, and it was his turn to start prowling restlessly about the room. "From all that I know of him he will be quite shattered, and at his age that will not be good for him. You are his heir, his favourite son – despite the fact that the two of you seldom if ever see eye to eye on anything. And all because of a drab – a lady of no account!"

He looked directly at the Marquis, as if daring him to challenge him to a duel, also, but Lord Capel merely smiled.

"Aren't you inclined to overlook something?" he asked, the smile creating a glimmer like starshine in his intensely dark eyes, fringed with eyelashes that were even longer and more luxuriant than Lady Fanny Bingham's.

"What?" Charles Cavendish replied.

"The possibility that Aintree might get me before I get him. He's a marksman with something of a reputation – even in these days when such things are inclined to be hushed up."

Charles made a gesture as if he discounted such a possibility.

"If he has a reputation, you are acknowledged to be singularly deadly. Have you forgotten what happened when you were only twenty-one? You made quite a mess of that Italian rake who affronted your sister, and everyone expected you to be carried home on a bier. The Duke got you out of that slight awkwardness, but I believe it was only after exacting a promise that you would never become involved in such a manner again. Yet here you are now about to turn your back on your promise – on your word to your father! Upon my word, Capel, I think this is a pretty shabby thing you are contemplating, and the lady isn't worth it. If nothing would induce you to marry her, why should you risk your life for her?"

"Because the risk, as you have been at such pains to point out, is small," the Marquis replied.

His friend made a gesture with his shoulders which indicated that his patience was wearing very thin.

"Very well," he said. "If you are really determined to go through with it –"

"I am."

"Then I had better leave you, and Bob and I will make the necessary arrangements. I shall return in about an hour, and after that I would advise you to get at least a couple of hours' sleep. No man is at his best after a wakeful night – and, in point of fact, I think you ought to – er –"

"Make my last will and testament? But it is already made," Lord Capel assured him smilingly. "However, there are one or two brief notes I think I might leave behind me – and perhaps some expressions of regret to my father."

His expression sobered, and for a brief moment a certain

faintly melancholy air of regret seemed to alter the curious harshness of his otherwise beautifully chiselled features.

"Poor father!" he exclaimed, almost softly. "If Bruce had been his heir life would have been so much pleasanter for him – bereft of the constant agitations which undoubtedly affect his heart. When my mama was alive she prevented many wild rumours from reaching his ears, but nowadays there is only Fanny . . . and she is almost as unpredictable as I am!"

"One can't help but feel a little sorry for the Duke of Coltsfoot," Charles Cavendish remarked, tight-lipped. "But at least, as you say, there is always Bruce –"

"And he succeeded in covering himself in so much glory during the recent campaign against Boney that his left leg has scarcely started to mend itself yet. He is nursing it at Hollowthorne, which I have lent to him for as long as he wants it. I had better put it on record that he can have it as a gift if I depart this life."

His expression, for a man endowed by nature with so many startling attributes in the way of good looks and a voice which was quite singularly attractive even when heavily overloaded with sarcasm, caused Cavendish to pause on his way to the door and stare at him rather hard.

"There is nothing I can say," he enquired, "that will cause you to change your mind?"

"Nothing, dear fellow."

"Then in addition to one or two other things you had better say your prayers. Aintree will not just try to wing you."

"I am well aware of that."

The Marquis bowed in a slightly mocking way, and the door closed on his friend. But the sound of his footsteps was still reaching them from the hall when Harriet literally sprang forth from her place of concealment.

"But you cannot possibly do this thing!" she cried. "I cannot possibly let you!"

The Marquis turned and confronted her, putting up his quizzing-glass.

"Good Gad!" he exclaimed. "Who in the world are you? And where, if I may put such a question, did you spring from?"

CHAPTER
FOUR

HAVING been forced to endure her own society for so long, and to remain entirely silent during that period, Harriet burst into speech. Never in her life had she suspected that she was capable of such eloquence.

"I am sorry, my lord, but I am not here for any purpose that concerns myself, and I am painfully aware that my presence here in your own home is a quite astonishing thing. And, indeed, some people might say that I have behaved outrageously ... you yourself, very probably, even when you have heard why I am here. I should not myself feel inclined to look upon such an intrusion lightly, but there are occasions – there are occasions, my lord, when one finds oneself with no other course open to one!"

"You alarm me," Lord Capel remarked in a smooth tone. "On how many occasions do you think you will find it necessary to hide behind my window curtains?"

She made a little gesture with her hand, appealing to him.

"My lord, you misunderstand me. I have no intention of concealing myself in this room again. But your butler must have acquainted you with my arrival this morning?"

"At what hour was that?" his lordship asked curiously.

"At about eleven of the clock, my lord."

"Then it would have been more than his life was worth to acquaint me of anything. I was safe in the arms of Morpheus at that hour, and Pauncefoot is only too well aware of the particular kind of dire retribution that would be his should he be so unwise – so extremely unwise! – as to attempt to arouse me under such circumstances."

"But he kept me waiting downstairs in the anteroom for fully another hour," Harriet protested. "I understood it was because he was making some attempt to, er – urge you to see me."

The Marquis shook his head slowly.

"Not my poor Pauncefoot. I would have had him shot at dawn for far less."

The unhappy turn of phrase seemed to amuse him.

"Instead of which it is I who am to be shot at dawn," he murmured. "Singular, do you not think?"

"I – I know that your lordship is contemplating something which has to be prevented."

"But not by you, I'm afraid, my dear Miss – er –? You must forgive me if I am a little curious about your identity. Pauncefoot may be well aware of it, but I, unhappily, am not."

"I am Harriet Yorke," Harriet told him, not thinking it in the least strange that he hadn't offered her a chair, since her method of calling upon him was a trifle unusual, and he had much on his mind besides. "I live in Sussex with Miss Verbena and Masters Robert and Ferdinand de Courcey, whose well-being I am responsible for – at least partially."

"I see," the Marquis murmured. "Sussex, you say? But who the deuce are Miss Verbena and Masters Robert and Ferdinand de Courcey? And why should I be troubled with their concerns at this time of night?"

"Because you are their guardian, my lord."

"I – am their guardian?" Lord Capel put up a white and shapely hand to his brow in seeming confusion. He frowned very noticeably, his well-marked black brows meeting above the bridge of his exceedingly well-formed nose. So far as he could recollect he had drunk very sparingly that evening, and

apart from that unpleasantness caused by a remark of Greville
Aintree's while they were playing cards, and his own reaction
to it, and the knowledge that he must write a letter to his
father, he had nothing very much else on his mind. But this
young woman was causing him a distinct feeling of uneasiness.
"Perhaps you will kindly explain to me how I can possibly
be a guardian to anyone apart from my dog Rufus, and his
latest bitch puppy?"

"Because you apparently agreed to accept them as your
wards when approached by Sir Willoughby de Courcey. He
died nearly six months ago."

The Marquis of Capel began to look as if some slight glim-
mering of understanding was dawning.

"Good God, yes," he agreed, "now you remind me of it . . .
And I do seem to remember that you wrote to me at some time
or other . . ."

"On three separate occasions, my lord," she said with the
very maximum amount of reproach in the words.

"And signed yourself Harriet Yorke. I wondered who the
hell you were –"

"I explained most carefully in the letters, if your lordship
had only read them."

The shock of his proposed meeting with Aintree in the mists
of an early April morning was passing slowly, and he began
to be aware of a decided feeling of resentment and irritation
because someone of whom he had never heard before, although
he might vaguely have noted her name on a letter, had
succeeded in doing a quite unpardonable thing, and was
putting him through some sort of inquisition here in his own
library. It was too much . . . And with the minutes ticking
away, and so much to be done. He recollected that she had
said something about preventing his meeting with Aintree,
and his ire rose further.

What an impertinent female! And a red-headed one, too!

He had disliked red-headed females all his life, and only jades possessed green eyes – as green as a cat's in the fireglow. Although, admittedly, in that drab pelisse and with those carroty curls escaping from beneath the brim of that decidedly unpretentious bonnet, she did not look like a jade.

He pushed a chair towards her.

"Sit down, Miss – er – Yorke," he invited. "This intrusion of yours is most unfortunate, since I have much on my mind – as you must be very fully aware, having shamelessly eavesdropped behind my curtains." Harriet turned rather pink, having very strong views herself on people who eavesdropped. "But the subject of the young de Courceys is one that I have faced up to on one or two occasions since their father, without any encouragement from me, I assure you, apparently left them in my charge. I will admit that I consulted my own lawyer on the matter, and he was all for making an issue of the thing; finding some means by which I could extricate myself from a situation which was not at all unlike becoming enmeshed in somebody else's web."

"But you must have been a very close friend of Sir Willoughby if you allowed him to prevail upon you to accept such a charge –"

"I give you my word I was nothing of the sort!" He flung a glance of such dislike at her that she began to feel a little alarmed, closeted as she was alone with him at that very late hour. "But I cannot go into the matter now, and moreover I do not intend to do so. I have other problems, much more pressing, on my mind!"

"But the young people's estate? Had you any idea that they are almost entirely without funds of their own?"

"Good God!" he exclaimed.

"And Verbena is growing out of her dresses, and Robert cannot even return to Oxford because there is no possibility of his being able to pay his fees! I think, my lord, that these are matters which most certainly you should pay some attention to."

"Do you mean to tell me I have control of their money, too?"

"Weren't you already aware of that?"

"I understood their father left something –" He flung away from her, in the direction of the massive desk in a corner of the room. He seated himself behind it, and groped for writing materials. "All this I will discuss with you on some other occasion."

"But I am leaving London tomorrow, and –"

"And what?" he asked, regarding her with complete cynicism.

"If – if you are to engage in this – this duel, we have no idea at all what – what might happen to you –"

"I have," he assured her. "I shall be sitting here at this desk at this hour tomorrow night and destroying the letters I now intend to write – if you will very kindly leave me alone in order that I may do so. The servants will have retired to bed, but if you have no very great objection to letting yourself out –"

"But your friend," she said hastily, rising and moving across the room until she stood at his elbow, "your friend, the gentleman who has just left, seemed to think there was no possibility that your adversary would – wing you. He seemed to think he would – kill you!"

"Unless I happen to kill him first!"

"But that would mean you would have to flee the country!"

"A somewhat poetic assessment of the opportunities open to me," he commented. He rested an elbow on the desk and leaned his chin on his hand, and regarded her with a somewhat tired air of making a supreme effort to be patient with her. "Will you go now, Miss Yorke, and if I am alive at this time tomorrow I will grant you a further interview."

"But I would prefer to see and talk with you when it is daylight. It would be a little less unconventional."

"Then you must accompany me to the spot where either I or my friend Aintree are to be despatched before our time. There will be several other people participating in the affair in order to make certain it is conducted on lines acceptable to gentlemen, if not to the mealy-minded who make the laws of our country, and from your point of view there will be nothing incriminatingly unconventional about it. We could always explain," with great dryness, "that my wards were not unnaturally anxious about me."

She was about to protest further that she would not enjoy being an onlooker at a duel, when the front door bell pealed with alarming loudness, and Lord Capel rose and urged her to take refuge again behind her curtain.

"This will be Charles returning, accompanied, I have no doubt, by another of my friends and well-wishers – on this occasion, at least," with some of the dryness he had used before. "Make sure that you remain well hidden, and whatever you hear do not interfere. That is an instruction I lay precisely upon you!"

When he returned to the library with Charles Cavendish and a young man wearing the uniform of the Coldstream Guards, all three of them were discussing the suitability of the contents of the long black case the young officer carried beneath his arm.

He set it down on the table in the library, and the three heads bent over it. On a bed of velvet, funereal in hue, lay a couple of handsomely mounted duelling pistols. Lord Capel lifted out one of them and balanced it on his hand. By his expression he obviously approved, and through her peep-hole near the window Harriet saw how the candle flames danced in the silver embellishments on the exquisitely slender weapon.

"These will do nicely," the Marquis said. "These will do very nicely!"

The detachment in his voice, apart from a faint note of admiration, amazed Harriet. Men, she thought, were utterly unlike women. A woman in such circumstances could not have behaved with such utter calmness. She might even have been growing a little hysterical as the dawn drew that much nearer.

"Thank you very much, Bob," the Marquis added. "You have done admirably."

Charles Cavendish glanced across at the desk, and said meaningly:

"You have been writing, Rick? I hope you have not very much more to do before getting a little sleep?"

"I have been trying to write one or two letters which I'm sure you would consider all-important," replied the Marquis, with a rather wry curve to his lips. "But I do not seem to be progressing with remarkable speed."

"Then make them as brief as possible." He laid a hand on his friend's shoulder. "After all, you may very well have to consign them to the wastepaper basket. And if you do not –"

"If I do not," Lord Capel took him up, looking him straight in the eye, "you will see to it that they are delivered?"

"Of course, Rick."

The young officer named Bob, who was wearing one of the most envied uniforms at that time, gazed at him commiseratingly.

"Wish you wouldn't do it, Rick," he said. "Wish you'd see sense. Damn it, man," throwing out his hands, "there's so very little point in it! Fellow's a cad, anyway, and one of these days some one else will put him out of the way if necessary. But not you!"

Richard Wendover, Marquis of Capel, merely smiled at him, still in a somewhat one-sided way.

"Have a drink," he invited, "before you depart." He assembled glasses on a tray, and poured from a decanter. "At what time will you call for me, Charles?"

Charles cocked an eye at the window behind a protective curtain of which Harriet was striving to make herself as small and insignificant as possible. She was a little alarmed when he walked to the window and, thrusting aside the companion curtain, glanced upwards at the sky, in which a few inquisitive stars seemed to be already paling.

"It will be broad daylight in another four hours," he said. "We do not wish to attract attention, so if we call for you in three hours' time — no; say two and a half — we shall be at the rendezvous in excellent time. Certainly there will be time enough."

"And if you need to be bled, Rick," young Captain Robert Markham said cheerfully, "we have the very man for the job. He will be there to attend to you."

"But it is my profound hope that no one will require to be bled," Charles Cavendish said seriously.

When they had left the Marquis called to Harriet to come out from behind the curtain. He was pouring a glass of Madeira, and he handed it to her.

"Drink this," he said. "I noted that you had been regaling yourself with ratafia, but this will sustain you rather better than that. I am going upstairs to my own room, and I shall write my letters there. I suggest that you make yourself as comfortable as possible in one of the chairs here, and I will see that you are called when Charles and Bob arrive."

"But it is all so extremely unconventional," she protested. "And what will they think when they — when they discover I was here all the time?"

The Marquis smiled mysteriously.

"What do men ever think about women? It is because one of them made a modest appeal to me — rather more than any other member of her sex has ever done – that I am setting forth to-morrow in the cold grey light of dawn to avenge what I considered an unnecessary slur on her reputation."

Harriet regarded him wide-eyed.

"But it will do her no good," she protested. "And if she has only a modest attraction for you . . .?"

"Ah, but no woman has ever had even a modest attraction for me before," he replied, and smiled at her quizzically. "Think what I might have been prepared to do if I had been wholeheartedly in love with her."

The evening – in fact, the whole day – had been an extremely unusual experience for Harriet, and she was beginning to feel a little confused . . . and by no means certain why she was not insisting on leaving there and then, and finding her way back to Paddington alone – and on foot if necessary. The explanation she offered to herself was her acute anxiety for the young de Courceys, but having had a certain amount of opportunity to reflect she was rather inclined to wonder whether it was nothing more nor less than pure obstinacy on her part that was making her behave as she never would have believed she could ever contemplate behaving.

She studied the Marquis more dubiously. A few sips of the Madeira had revived her a little, but she was extremely tired, and in the dim candlelight her eyes were no longer focusing as well as they might – or that was her own impression. The Marquis's face looked pale and grim, and he was leaning rather heavily on the table as if he, too, were tired.

"You could do no more for any woman than to lay down your life for her," she said a trifle huskily.

"Couldn't I?" He downed another glass of wine in a single gulp, and then poured himself another. "But at least that has its advantages over offering her marriage. I have always eschewed marriage."

Harriet regarded him with very wide open eyes indeed. She

could not help but decide in her own mind that he was more than a little mad. Indeed, she thought he must be very mad indeed if he could make such a choice between living and dying. At the very least he must be extraordinarily quixotic.

"I'm afraid I quite fail to understand the rationality of such a statement as that," she told him.

He smiled.

"By that you mean you are not entirely certain I have a rational mind. Well, very likely I have not." He tilted his glass in her direction. "And what about you, you coppery-haired, green-eyed, extraordinarily intrepid – wench? I find your excessive obstinacy, and the determination with which you tracked me to my lair today, commendable if one regards your activities in a certain light, but otherwise quite irrational. You could have come to tremendous harm if I had been somewhat otherwise than what I am – and very much preoccupied with other matters! Did that never occur to you?"

"Yes," she admitted, "it did. But the situation was so serious that I had no other course open to me," she added, with a simplicity and straightforwardness which seemed to make their appeal to him.

"Gad!" he exclaimed. "You really are an astonishing member of your sex. Something tells me you would never give up easily, and I believe you would fight like the devil if you encountered serious opposition. Do you enjoy having something in common with the devil, Miss Yorke?"

"My father was known as Devil Yorke," she answered.

"Indeed?" He frowned suddenly, in an effort to recollect. "Was he in the Navy, at the Battle of Copenhagen, one of Nelson's captains who covered himself in glory during that operation and created quite a stir at the Admiralty for some time afterwards?"

She nodded.

"Then I trust he received his proper reward and died full of honours and material benefits?" with a somewhat questioning glance at her shabby pelisse.

"On the contrary, my lord," she admitted, "he died a very poor man, but that was not because his country refused to acknowledge what was due to him, but because he had an unerring facility for dissipating wealth as fast as he acquired it."

"Which explains the reason why you appear to be a kind of watchdog to the de Courcey family?"

"In part, it does," she agreed.

"But only in part? Don't tell me you actually enjoy looking after other people's brats?"

Without waiting for her answer he flung away to a far corner, took a turn or two about the room, and then returned to his desk and gathered together a sufficient supply of writing materials.

"Goodnight, Miss Yorke," he said. "Or, rather, I should say Good morning, since the first cock has already started to crow ... Get what little sleep you can, and be ready to leave the instant I wake you."

"And who will wake you, my lord?"

"My man will receive his instructions before I attempt to forget my troubles in temporary oblivion. I trust you will not find the library chairs too hard."

CHAPTER
FIVE

HARRIET passed the remainder of the night in acute discomfort, sleeping only fitfully, and was finally awakened in the dawn light to find Lord Capel tugging at her elbow. He directed her to a room on the first floor of the house where she could make use of a pitcher of water and some fresh towels; and afterwards a little maidservant, roused by his lordship's valet, carried to the library a tray of chocolate of which they both partook.

Then a carriage rolled up outside, and Charles Cavendish alighted and ran up the steps. The Marquis was waiting for him, and he thrust Harriet out on to the steps and urged her to descend as quickly and quietly as possible to the carriage. The two other gentlemen, both muffled to the eyes in many-collared capes, gaped at her in astonishment, but Lord Capel introduced her simply and curtly as "Miss Yorke, governess to my wards."

It became immediately clear that the others suspected some sort of mental derangement where the Marquis was concerned, but not unnaturally they said nothing. Captain Markham, never known to be impolite, and certainly not when the lady had red curls and clear cheeks, accorded her a brief, military bow and then placed her in a corner of the carriage. The others accepted the vacant seats in the carriage.

Although so early in the day the atmosphere was remarkably clear. There were no dawn mists obscuring the landscape or slowly dispersing clouds concealing the clarity of the morning sky. The latter was palely blue and exquisite, a flush of rose low down on the horizon heralding the approach of the sun. One or two stars still gazed at their reflections in patches of still water, but otherwise the night had passed.

Harriet had no idea at all of their destination, but it seemed to her that they travelled a remarkable distance in a remarkably short space of time. The streets of prosperous-looking London houses gave place to meaner and far from salubrious streets, and then they were out on a winding road which was bordered by woods and meadows, and finally became a road cutting across a common where the trees stood sentinel-like against the sky. Here, in the shadow of one of these groups of trees, the carriage came to rest, and a little cluster of gentlemen who had obviously arrived before them stood watching as the steps were put down and they alighted from the carriage.

For the first time Harriet realised that it was very cold. The gentlemen were all well protected against the sharpness of the atmosphere, but her light woollen pelisse felt extremely inadequate as she took up her position beneath a spreading oak, and the dew-soaked grass beneath her feet wet her shoes in no time at all.

"Whatever you do keep well clear of anything that is happening," the Marquis warned her, "and do not interfere under any circumstances."

After which he left her to her own devices. She realised that from that moment she was banished altogether from his mind, and the stern realities of the business that lay ahead occupied all his thoughts and attention. He did not look precisely pale, but he could have had a little more colour, and the set of his mouth was intensely grim.

The other little band of gentlemen provided quite a contrast. They were all grouped closely together, surrounding their central figure as if to offer him what protection they could until the very last moment, and that central figure, unlike the

Marquis and his two friends, appeared to be extraordinarily light-hearted. He was not a tall man, but there was an elegance about him, and when he began to strip down to his fine cambric shirt and breeches the litheness of his movements, and a certain grace which attended them, began to make it clear that whatever else he might be, he would be very nimble on his feet. And although she could not overhear the conversation Harriet quickly realised that Mr. Greville Aintree was delivering himself of a number of smart quips and jokes which had his supporters guffawing loudly at one stage.

The Marquis, on the other hand, was silent, and neither of his supporters appeared to have much to say.

When the doctor arrived in a hired chaise he went straight up to them and the conversation from that moment on was brief and very much to the point.

Harriet, who had never expected to experience anything in the least like this in the whole of her life, began to feel distinctly apprehensive. She knew so little of the Marquis of Capel – and certainly nothing that reflected very much in his favour – that it would have been quite untrue to say that she was worried on his account, apart from the awkwardness his demise might occasion to the de Courceys; but she knew absolutely nothing at all about the other man, and it was difficult to be in the least partisan. She only knew that she wished the whole affair over as quickly as possible, and that her wet shoes were not directing a chill right up into the very heart of her being, and that a wedge of geese flying overhead would cease their noise so that she could hear what was going on.

When the two seconds approached one another and conferred for a short while she realised that she had not very much longer to wait. The Marquis was standing alone by this time, looking aloof and disdainful, as well as very shapely in an altogether masculine manner in his fine white silk shirt, a little open at the neck, with his thick black hair curling crisply in the morning light. He was watching his second pacing out the ground, and he knew that the moment was near.

The case of pistols had been presented, and each man had accepted and carefully weighed his weapon. Robert Markham had stepped back and joined Harriet in the shade of the trees, but Charles Cavendish was the man who would call the count of ten, then drop the white handkerchief which would signal the moment to fire.

Harriet found herself swallowing nervously, and her hands were clenched inside her gloves. Beside her Captain Markham was rigidly still. Harriet whispered to him:

"Do you think they will really try and kill one another...?"

"S-sh!"

Harriet felt as if a wave of panic, and nothing less, welled over her. Greville Aintree was smiling complacently right up until the last moment, but the Marquis's expression was positively murderous. Harriet became convinced that he intended to despatch his man without compunction, and the thought of the smile on Aintree's face being wiped off in a moment in such a horrible manner brought about such a state of revulsion that, as she realised afterwards, it blotted out all reasoning. Aintree was not even personally known to her, and she thought that if she had enjoyed the benefit of his acquaintance it might have proved a very dubious benefit indeed; but, since he was a fellow human being, and without a doubt he was in the most acute danger...

She darted forward, as far as she was aware without the least conscious volition, just as the handkerchief was raised aloft and every eye was upon it. By the time it fluttered to the ground the Marquis's arm had been violently jolted and there were horrified shouts and protests. And then Harriet was thrust rudely aside and the Marquis's friends supported him on both sides. The doctor was already kneeling beside the still figure of Greville Aintree, staining the grass with his blood the prescribed distance away. Aintree's little group of friends, too shocked to move in his direction, looked as if they simply could not believe the evidence of their eyes.

And in the clear morning light two puffs of smoke, like balls of morning mist, ascended to the tranquil blue of the sky.

Harriet covered her face with her gloved hands. What had she done? What dreadful thing had she been guilty of?

No one was prepared to glance in her direction. They were all too preoccupied, with the exception of the two principals in this affair, one of whom was standing between his friends and staring almost stupidly and quite unbelievingly at the sinister immobility of the man he had intended should walk away from this secluded spot with nothing more than a salutary flesh wound to show for his early rising. And as for the victim, the sprucely dressed gentleman who had betrayed so much cheerfulness – even if it was a little unseemly – such a short while before ... Well, he was beyond taking even the smallest amount of interest in anyone who had witnessed his sudden collapse, let alone anyone who had contributed to it.

The Marquis spoke thickly between his teeth.

"I never intended ... Is he dead?"

Captain Markham replied in very much the same tone of voice.

"It's impossible to be certain, Rick, but I'll find out, if you're sure you can manage with Charles's support only? You're bleeding like a pig, you know, but I don't think it's anything serious – "

"Devil take you, man, of course it's not serious!" The Marquis wrenched himself out of his hands with a kind of repressed fury. "Did you think I thought I'd been killed, too, and all because that little fool there refused to obey an order?"

The sheer malevolence of the glance he cast at the "little fool" in question drove the few remaining shreds of colour out of her face. Nevertheless she tottered towards him.

"I'm so sorry, Lord Capel! I'm so dreadfully sorry! I really cannot understand what came over me – "

"Then don't try," he advised her icily. "Don't do anything but stay over there, where I can't see you."

"But you must understand that I didn't intend – " And then her eyes widened dramatically as they took in the full horror and implication of his blood-soaked sleeve. "But you're wounded!" she exclaimed, her voice growing a little faint as if the sight of that fine white shirt being so dramatically discoloured was a little too much for her feminine endurance. "You really are badly hurt! You must allow me to assist you – "

"Stay over there," he ordered, closing his eyes and gritting his teeth as fiery pains shot up and down his arm. "Don't come an inch nearer!"

"But I know quite a lot about dealing with emergencies . . ." Which was true enough, as her father had more than once arrived home from one of his affrays with a wound which refused to heal, and with which she had had to deal conscientiously. "At least I can staunch the blood – "

Charles Cavendish intervened in an urgent tone.

"Pray don't excite him, Miss Yorke," he begged. "You can do no good." He could have added: "You have already done quite enough!"

Captain Markham returned, accompanied by a suitably sober-faced physician, who insisted upon examining the Marquis before answering his urgent questions.

"How is he? Will he live?"

"I don't think we need worry overmuch about the extent of the damage done to your arm, my lord," he said in as soothing a tone as he could muster under such circumstances. "It is no more than a rather nasty flesh wound. . . ."

"Yes, yes," the Marquis replied, making an impatient gesture. "But Aintree? What of Aintree?"

"He is alive," the doctor replied very soberly. "But that is as much as I can say."

The Marquis drew in his breath almost painfully.

"Thank God!" he exclaimed.

"Naturally, his situation is critical," the doctor added, with rather more of a note of criticism – not to say actual disapproval – in his voice this time. "The ball penetrated his shoulder, but it has done some damage in the area of his right lung, which as you will be aware is a vital area and could cause us some trouble. At the moment he is unconscious, and it is better that he should remain so until I have got him somewhere where I can operate. And if the ball is removed fairly expeditiously – and the loss of blood is not excessive. . . ."

Lord Capel nodded, his face very white indeed.

"I understand," he said quietly. "And I would like to make it clear that any expenses incurred must be my affair entirely, and no effort must be spared to save him. Will you give me your word that you will do everything in your power?"

The doctor bowed.

"I will, my lord. I will do my very best." He shrugged his shoulders slightly. "But beyond that it is not entirely up to me. . . . Your lordship will understand that, of course?"

Once again the Marquis nodded.

"You saw what happened?" he said curtly.

"I did indeed, my lord," he replied, without glancing in Harriet's direction.

"Damnation!" the Marquis of Capel exclaimed, and turned and walked stiffly in the direction of his carriage.

His two friends followed, and Harriet, although receiving no invitation to do so, trailed humbly behind them. She noticed that Lord Capel barely glanced at the man lying unconscious on the ground, with his stricken friends kneeling beside him, although they passed within a few feet of the unhappy little group on the way to the carriage. Harriet, on the other hand, felt as if something impelled her to halt beside the victim and bestow upon him a glance of the utmost compassion, and when she saw how completely inert he was, and how waxen his face, she could not prevent herself from dropping to her own knees beside him and enquiring of his companions whether there was anything at all she could do to help.

But from their frozen expressions she gathered that they would prefer not to know her.

"Thank you, madam," one replied. "But Dr. Groves has already done all that is possible in such a situation as this. We are entirely in his hands."

Harriet nodded, and rose quietly to her feet, realising to the full as she did so how outrageously she had behaved. And yet all that she had intended was thoroughly admirable, could they but have understood her motives to secure the life of Greville Aintree, when it appeared to be desperately threatened, and prevent Lord Capel becoming a murderer! And if her concern with Lord Capel had been her primary motive, the thought of her three charges in Sussex had seemed a sufficient excuse.

And yet now she was far from being sure. She was desperately certain that she had behaved in a completely unforgivable manner.

She cast one more glance at Greville Aintree, staining the short, sweet grass of the common with the steady flow of his blood, and then heeded the urgent voice of Captain Markham.

"Miss Yorke," he called, "we are anxious to get the Marquis back to his house as quickly as possible. Will you please not cause us any delay."

"I am coming at once," she replied, and moved hurriedly in the direction of the carriage.

CHAPTER
SIX

ONCE inside the carriage Harriet allowed herself to be wedged between the captain and the austere but handsome Mr. Cavendish, while Lord Capel was disposed as comfortably as possible on the opposite seat. For the first half mile or so of the journey he remained completely silent, lying back with his eyes closed and his mouth tightly compressed, as if he was suffering a good deal. And it was only when he opened his eyes and looked directly across at her that Harriet realised, as she saw the glitter of cold fury between his thick black eyelashes, that the physical part of his ordeal was not that which was causing the greater disturbance to him at that moment.

The line of his lips was positively frightening, and the cold glitter filled her with no small amount of alarm.

"I hope you are satisfied, Miss Yorke," he said, "with your performance today."

Without any real hope of appeasing his anger she made an attempt.

"I have told you, my lord," she replied, in the most abject of tones, "that I am so truly sorry for what I have done that I cannot possibly express how badly I feel about it. I have no certainty that I would not do it again in similar circumstances, but I know I behaved atrociously, and as a result a man's life lies in the balance."

"If he dies, you will have the satisfaction of knowing yourself his murderer," the Marquis informed her with icy cruelty.

Charles Cavendish moved protestingly on the seat beside Harriet, and frowned across at the Marquis.

"You cannot, if you wish to be entirely fair to Miss Yorke, make such a statement as that, Rick," he offered in a quiet but firm tone, while he smiled unexpectedly at Harriet. His latent chivalry sent a little flood of warmth surging about her heart. "Her behaviour was no more than one might have expected from a member of her sex. It is quite clear that her only intention was to prevent you doing serious harm to Aintree."

"Instead of which she has got the fellow killed – or as good as," Lord Capel said with a curl of his remarkably handsome upper lip. "And I suppose it never even occurred to her that *I* might have been the one left behind there on the common!"

Harriet shivered uncontrollably.

"Oh, no!" she protested. "It was simply that I – I didn't really think!"

And for the first time she did think how utterly disastrous that would have been for the de Courceys.

His lordship bowed to her ironically, and winced immediately afterwards because the unwise movement caused him considerable discomfort.

"You are too kind, ma'am," he said to her witheringly. "And it does incline one to wonder what precise action you would have taken if you *had* thought!"

Captain Markham, who had been gazing out of the carriage window in an unseeing way, barely aware of the familiar landmarks that were gliding past on either hand, or the increasing evidence that they were drawing nearer and nearer to London and their ultimate destination, St. James's Square, with every turn of the wheels, rounded suddenly upon his three fellow-travellers and accused them of wasting valuable time.

With the utmost resolution he announced:

"There is no point in blaming Miss Yorke for what has happened. It has happened, and there's nothing we can do about it. But you, Rick! Now there's a problem we have to deal with, and little enough time to do it in. If Aintree dies it'll be a devilish awkward situation – devilish awkward! Those friends of his will be out for your blood like a pack of hounds, and they'll be on to you before you can say 'It's a damn fine morning!' unless you go to ground. And, hell and damnation, Rick, it won't be no fine morning for you if they catch up with you – it'll be a devilish gloomy day!"

"Thank you very much for such a comforting expression of your personal opinion, Bob," his lordship said with languor and a very great deal of dryness. He added, "But so far as we know Aintree isn't dead yet."

Markham shook his head at him.

"I wouldn't count on his surviving if I were you, Rick. The last I saw of him stretched out on that blasted heath he was certainly as good as dead, and I don't think that fellow Groves thought he was going to work any miracles when he started hacking away at that bullet of yours. I know you offered to recompense him handsomely if he achieved a miracle, but I thought his expression was pretty glum."

"I'm afraid that's perfectly true, Rick," Cavendish echoed his friend's sentiments in a very sober voice indeed.

"So?" the Marquis said, wishing he had a bottle of laudanum somewhere about his person, and wondering why a little group of trees on a nearby knoll appeared to be wavering most uncertainly despite his best endeavours to focus them.

"There's only one thing I can suggest," the captain responded earnestly, bending forward a little the better to impress the Marquis with the soundness of his reasoning. "We can't have you turning up in St. James's Square, and Pauncefoot turning pea-green at the sight of all that blood – to say nothing of all the errand boys in the district congregating on your doorstep to watch you being assisted into your house. Not if you're to go to ground until the whole thing's cooled off a little...." He paused, as if preparing himself to meet a considerable amount of opposition, and already detecting signs in the Marquis's face of positive mutiny. "You know my rooms in Albemarle Street? You've dined there on several occasions."

"Of course I know your rooms," Lord Capel replied pettishly. "But I can't say I've ever enjoyed your dinners."

The captain decided to overlook the ungraciousness of such an admission, and continued:

"Nevertheless, my housekeeper, who is also my landlady, is a woman of discretion and sound common sense, and she would be unlikely to bother you if you moved in for a short time. The rooms are comfortable enough, and you could remain hidden there for as long as we deem it necessary. I could move in with my sister and her brood in Berkeley Square. Her husband's hardly ever sober, so he won't really notice, and I haven't seen much of any of them since Waterloo. You won't be putting me about ... I find her brats diverting, and it's high time I took them about and bought them a few presents and things like that. Took on the role of uncle, don't you know?"

"I don't," Lord Capel replied feebly.

"Well, what do you say? It's better than Charles's place, because his man is forever on the watch and would smell a rat as soon as he set eyes on you, and in any case Charles would find it difficult to move out. If you say the word I'll order the coachman to stop and tell him to avoid St. James's Square like the plague and make for Albemarle Street."

It took a great deal more argument than this to convince the injured man that he had virtually no alternative to his friend's highly considerate and practical suggestion. And in the end he gave in ungraciously and only made one stipulation, and that was that his man Fetcham should be brought to him with as little delay as possible, and without alerting or alarming any of the other occupants of the house in St. James's Square. When the carriage stopped in Albemarle Street he declined to allow himself to be assisted to the pavement, and strode into the house and up the stairs to the sitting-room on the first floor with the vigour of a man in very fine fettle. It was only when he saw the inadequacy of the settee in the sitting-room that he turned through the door into the bedroom and collapsed on the bed. Harriet, who had followed the party into the house – once again without being invited – moved immediately to his side.

"Brandy," she called urgently. "Will someone please bring the Marquis some brandy?"

She was well aware that raw spirit was the last thing a man in his condition should receive, but as he appeared more dead than alive as he lay sprawled on the bed she could think of nothing else that was likely to revive him.

A short time later, propped up by pillows and with a certain amount of colour returned to his face, his lordship uttered a grudging "thank you" to Miss Yorke. After she had taken a good look at his wound, it struck her as by no means the kind which anyone as unskilled as herself should be called upon to deal with; but at the same time she understood the unwillingness of the Marquis's friends to call in a local doctor.

There might be awkward questions to answer, and it could do harm to the Marquis himself. The whole object of taking over Captain Markham's apartment was to prevent anyone asking awkward questions.

"Don't worry," the Marquis urged them at last, becoming increasingly petulant as the argument over what was the best thing to be done in the circumstances was waged over his head – quite literally, in fact, since he was lying completely supine throughout the better part of it. It was only when he found he could not endure it any longer that he struggled into a sitting position. "I have no feeling that I am actually going to die, although it might simplify matters all round if I could be so obliging as to do so. You could then have me smuggled down the back stairs and interred somewhere locally with as little delay as possible and as decently as you could contrive. But unhappily for you two gentlemen, associates of my bosom, I am extraordinarily resistant to pressures upon me, and with the help of Fetcham, when he arrives, I shall survive. He has dug more bullets out of wounded men than I have tied cravats, and if you want to know all about it I suggest you question him when he arrives. He was with the fifty-second at Orthez."

Captain Markham drew an instant breath of relief, and even Charles Cavendish's expression brightened.

"In that case, Rick," he said, "perhaps you will forgive me if I leave you now. I have an engagement which it would be excessively impolite of me to ignore, and it appears there is little more I can actually do for you at this present."

"There is nothing," his lordship assured him, anxious to be left alone.

"And I," Markham spoke up swiftly, being comfortably aware that a greater degree of urgency attached to his reason for leaving the wounded man to his devices, "have to prepare my sister for my descent upon her, and to acquaint your man Fetcham with your need of him here. So I trust you will forgive me too, Rick, if I do not delay any longer?"

Lord Capel acknowledged this with a very faint movement of his hand. Then, as the other two men looked somewhat awkwardly at Harriet as if by no means certain they had a right to impose on her any further, but hoping fervently that she would volunteer to remain with the invalid until his manservant could take over the duty, a faint glimmer of amusement appeared in the eyes of Richard Wendover, and he made an unexpected but quite open appeal to her.

"Well, Miss Yorke?" he said, those over-bright eyes watching her with a certain amount of relish. "Are you going to abandon me, too, having reduced me to such a parlous state? Or do you propose to do your womanly duty and stay and hold my hand until Fetcham arrives?"

Harriet ignored the suggestion about holding his hand, and replied – having already made up her mind that there was no other course open to her – that she would remain. But only, she added firmly, until such time as he was unlikely to be left alone.

"Of course," his lordship agreed smoothly. "Of course! Otherwise Bob's landlady might have some reason to object!"

"Oh, she won't trouble you," Markham assured him. "She'll stay out of sight unless you need her, and if you do need her just ring the bell." He smiled appreciatively as well as gratefully at Harriet. "Then she'll come at once. She's a devilish fine, sensible sort of a woman – and the best cook in London, despite what Rick says!"

Lord Capel snorted.

"If I have to endure both her food and her company I shall devise prompt plans to remove myself from such unwanted ministrations," he assured them all with a sudden burst of energetic emphasis. "I give you my word on that!"

Harriet approached the bed and laid a cool hand on his forehead.

"If I were you, my lord," she advised sensibly, "I would lie very still and conserve your strength. You must remember that any unwise movement is likely to cause your wound to start bleeding afresh."

The other two tiptoed hastily from the room, very much

relieved that they were making their escape and convinced that Harriet had the makings of a remarkably fine nurse. And for a young woman with such enchanting curls and remarkably fine eyes that was a quite extraordinary thing.

CHAPTER
SEVEN

THE MORNING wore slowly away, and it was late afternoon before Fetcham put in an appearance. During those hours, which seemed to Harriet to drag interminably, the patient lay on the bed and slept intermittently, and when he was not sleeping he complained bitterly of the pretty pass to which he had been brought, of the stupidity of women, and the unreliability of his friends.

"What do you suppose they are doing?" he asked constantly, staring up into Harriet's face with his feverishly bright dark eyes. "Fetcham would come at once if he was made aware of my situation, but since he has not come Bob must have been unforgivably negligent. That sister of his ... She's an empty-headed scatterbrain if you like! She's probably got him crawling all over the nursery floor, tempting the little ones with bonbons, while I lie here practically at death's door ..."

"You are not at death's door." Harriet spoke with a good deal of firmness, because this was not the first time he had made such an assertion. "You are not even close to death's door. You have sustained a nasty wound, and I suspect you are suffering from mounting fever; and when your man arrives – "

"But he hasn't arrived! And, in any case, whose fault is it that I am suffering from what you call mounting fever?" he demanded, raising himself on his uninjured elbow and glaring at her. "Whose fault but yours? *Yours*, you red-headed, green-eyed, disobedient, ill-omened, disaster-procuring female? And tell me," he added, lying back in a more relaxed attitude on the bed, "what precisely was your reason for jogging my elbow? Did you really wish to see me killed?"

"No, of course not!" she exclaimed hurriedly, in horror. The expression in her eyes convinced him that he had shocked her profoundly. "Why should I wish to see you killed, my lord? I hardly know you, for one thing," she pointed out.

"True," he admitted, "but you could have been acting in the interests of those de Courcey brats. You thought perhaps that if I was out of the way –"

"I thought nothing of the kind! I assure you, my lord, I thought nothing – *nothing* of the kind!" She felt herself turn slightly cold because he could even think such a thing of her. "I only thought that – that perhaps I could prevent you, whom I understood to be an almost fatal shot, from killing – from killing –"

"One of the most experienced and deadly duellists in Europe?" He lay gazing up at her cynically. "Because that is what he is! The unfortunates whose days he has abruptly terminated make up quite an impressive list! I was very well aware of it when I issued my challenge to him last night. And perhaps that was one excellent reason why I issued my challenge. But I did not intend to kill him!"

"Then what purpose was there in your meeting him at all?"

"Ah, there speaks the daughter of Devil Yorke!" A faint relish stole about the curves of his handsome mouth, and he even bestowed upon her a look of mild approval. "Why, endanger your own life if there is no rhyme or reason? Why do anything quite so foolish, even reprehensible, with a young lady like yourself on hand to reverse the possibilities! And in all truth I must admit I cannot give you a concise answer as to why I took such particular exception to his vulgarity last night."

"Except that it concerned a lady? A friend?"

"Yes; a lady – and a friend!"

"And you would have done as much for any other – friend?"

A glittering, amused smile appeared beneath his heavy lids.

"It is – possible."

"I doubt it, my lord. I think the lady must mean more to you than – than perhaps you yourself are prepared to recognise . . ."

"Or perhaps I was simply foxed?"

"If you mean drunk, my lord, then in my opinion you were not at all drunk."

"And you have a large experience of drunken gentlemen?"

"Of course not," and she actually blushed a little.

He eyed the blush approvingly.

"Do you know, Miss Yorke," he said suddenly, conversationally, "you are a most attractive young lady? Apart from being the daughter of the devil you have quite a few other things to commend you . . . And suffering acutely, as I am, it is amazing I can make such an admission! You attempt to interrupt the progress of a duel, you take on the nursing of a sick man, you are prepared to argue on any and every occasion – "

"No, sir," she assured him, quietly, laying a hand gently once more on his brow. "I am merely trying to keep your lordship in a reasonably calm frame of mind while you await the attentions of your manservant. To divert you is important if it prevents you fretting overmuch. And if Fetcham does not arrive soon I really will have to call a physician – "

"You will do nothing of the kind." He caught hold of her hand and held it tightly. "Fetcham will be here at any moment now," which was an optimistic attitude he had not shown before. "But do you know of one thing about which I am now reasonably certain?"

"No, my lord?" She gazed at him in an enquiring way.

"If you had not jogged my elbow as you did, with the intention of preserving Aintree's life for him, *I* might now be dead! I might now be very dead indeed! For had you not jogged my arm that ball, which was intended for my heart, would have found its mark, instead of merely burying itself in my arm. So you see, Miss Yorke, that although you may well be responsible for the demise of Aintree, you are the daughter of the devil to whom I owe my life?"

"Oh, no!" she gasped – not because she was shocked at having saved him, but horrified by the extent of the danger to which he had come so close. "Oh, *no*!" she repeated.

The Marquis of Capel smiled.

"That is what I think," he said. "And indeed I am pretty sure of it."

Voices sounded on the stairs – the voice of Captain Markham's landlady, and what must without doubt be the voice of the Marquis's valet. Slightly raised, and obviously prepared to engage in altercation on the smallest provocation, it was insisting on its owner being shown upstairs to the captain's rooms with the minimum amount of delay.

"Of course, sir," the landlady replied, a faint note of awe in her tones as if she was greatly impressed by this very fine example of a very fine gentleman's gentleman. Yet when the door was opened, and Fetcham actually appeared in the bedroom – encumbered by such an extraordinary assortment of luggage that he found it rather difficult to negotiate the somewhat narrow entrance to the room – Harriet was amazed because he was such a slight and insignificant little man, wearing a distinct expression of anxiety, and with a somewhat harassed expression besides as if he had recently been put to no small amount of personal inconvenience.

He slammed the door smartly on the landlady, thereby ensuring that she saw nothing at all of the illustrious occupant of the bedroom, and advanced to the side of the bed with his many burdens still clutched to his minute person.

"Sorry, m'lord," he gasped, plainly out of breath, "but I couldn't get here no sooner on account of it being a bit awkward to get all this stuff out o' the 'ouse without Pauncefoot wantin' to know where I was takin' it. He was hanging about in the hall, and James, too, and I had to smuggle it out the back way – "

"Yes, yes," the Marquis replied peevishly, "but even so you've taken an unconscionable time getting here. Didn't Captain Markham make it clear to you that the situation was urgent?"

"Oh, yes, m'lord." Fetcham wiped his brow with a violently spotted handkerchief, and stared across the bed with open curiosity at Harriet. "He did that, m'lord, and at first I thought it was one of his jokes – you gettin' the worst of it! I just couldn't believe it, knowing how handy you are with any sort of firearm. It must have been one of your bad days, m'lord." He bent over the victim and, as Harriet had so frequently done in the past few hours, laid his hand on his forehead. He frowned. "You've got a regular fever, me lord. I'll have to have a look at that arm of yours."

"Then bring me a very large brandy first," ordered the Marquis. "Very large!"

But Fetcham shook his head.

"From the smell of your breath, m'lord, you've had more than enough of that stuff already," he offered it as his opinion. "But afterwards we'll see."

The bright, birdlike glances of open curiosity he was continually shooting at Harriet caused Lord Capel to explain her presence in as brief and pettish a way as he knew how.

"You can trust Miss Yorke, Fetcham," he assured him. "She's not likely to faint if you open me up and flood the room with my blood. But, on the other hand, she'll give you a good set-down if you do anything she disapproves of."

Far from arousing any natural antipathy in Fetcham, this

recommendation appeared to satisfy the manservant. He nodded at Harriet in an unreservedly pleasant manner, said: "In that case, miss, I'm glad to know you," and ordered her to get a grasp of the Marquis's free hand in case he tried being awkward while the bandage was being removed. And later, while Fetcham went to open up a small case of surgical instruments which he had brought with him and selected those he needed with infinite care, and the nasty raw wound in the Marquis's arm was exposed to view, Harriet urged the recumbent figure to avert his eyes from the unpleasantness of the sight, and once again earned the approbation of Fetcham.

"That's right, miss, keep his heart up!" he approved. "It's amazin' how gentlemen can turn faint at the sight of a hole in their own arm, though they don't mind makin' holes in other people's," with the very mildest note of rebuke in his voice as he looked down at his master. "And from what Captain Markham said to me this morning the other gentleman in this case ain't feeling exactly happy at this moment."

Lord Capel gritted his teeth.

"Get on with it, Fetcham," he urged.

"Very good, m'lord, I'm getting on with it," Fetchem replied.

When it was all over, Harriet released the Marquis's fingers and felt herself becoming a little faint. Lord Capel's assertion that she would refrain from showing weakness whatever occurred was not entirely deserved, and the aftermath of the manservant's extraordinarily skilled probing, which resulted in the final extraction of the bullet, was enough to shatter the confidence of the most stout-hearted young woman of her years. While the Marquis was actually in need of her support, and the bruising effect of his hold on her actually numbed her fingers, she was not in any danger of sliding into a little heap on the carpet; but once it was over, the patterns in the carpet began to waver before her eyes, and as for Lord Capel's face – white and drawn and a little blue about the lips – it was for one moment blotted out of her comprehension.

"Fetcham," his lordship called faintly, "you'd better give Miss Yorke a tot of brandy. She looks to me as if she needs it."

"Just what I was about to do, m'lord," the imperturbable Fetcham replied, and put a wineglass into Harriet's hand. She gulped at it gratefully, and then choked a little.

"I'm so sorry," she gasped. "I'm not used to – to spirit."

"Nor assistin' at operations o' this kind, I'm sure, miss," he replied, bestowing upon her an almost paternal glance of approval. "But takin' all that into account, and makin' proper allowance for you being a female, I must say I wouldn't have minded havin' you at my elbow on more than one occasion when I was doin' similar things at Orthez. And having said that, I've said a good deal, believe me, miss!"

"Hear, hear," came somewhat sarcastically, but in not quite such a faint tone, from the bed. "You've won the accolade of Fetcham's full and unreserved approval, Miss Yorke," the Marquis told her.

Taking another, rather more furtive, sip at her brandy, Harriet set the glass down and approached the bed once more.

"And you, my lord?" she asked. "How are you feeling?"

"Very much as you were feeling just now – only worse," the Marquis told her.

"But the bullet is out, and the wound is quite healthy. You will recover very soon," Harriet assured him, making fluttering movements with her hands and straightening his pillows.

The Marquis smiled up at her.

"I really am grateful," he said a little huskily.

"And now, I'm afraid, I will have to leave you."

But he caught her arm and held it with bruising fingers.

"You'll do nothing of the kind!" he astonished her by telling her. "If you think I've survived all that I have just suffered to lose my nurse at a moment when I am sadly in need of all the tender care and ministering she can provide me with, then you will, Miss Yorke, have to think again I'm afraid, I should have a relapse immediately if you left me to the mercies of Fetcham in this dismal apartment," glancing around it as if he had conceived a quite disproportionate dislike of it and its very obvious comforts. "I intend to leave here at the very first moment that we can put some practical plan into action, and you, Miss Yorke, will go with me! Come here, Fetcham!"

Fetcham approached the bed, and waited for his master's orders.

"Tell that woman downstairs to send up a tray of tea and something light to eat for Miss Yorke, and while she is recovering her energies you must collect what luggage she has deposited at some address she has been staying at in Paddington bring it back here to Albemarle Street. After that you must arrange for a carriage to be here around about the hour of midnight, when it should be safe to set forth, and Bob Markham's inquisitive landlady will have retired to bed in her curlers, and we will make for Hollowthorne, where my brother Bruce will be the only human we need contact who will not endanger us – or, rather, me! And I think he'll be able to vouch for his physician, too, if I should need one."

Fetcham regarded him quizziclly.

"And you really think you'll feel up to it, m'lord? Such a journey as that! After all that poking and probing you 'ad to put up with just now?"

"Of course I'll feel up to it," Lord Capel assured him impatiently, his impatience bringing rather a hectic flush to his cheeks. "I have no alternative course open to me."

"And the young lady?" One of Fetcham's eyebrows cocked upwards quite comically, and Harriet felt a flush rising to her cheeks also. "Won't it be rather like kidnapping her, m'lord? Especially if she don't agree!"

"I really must return to Paddington," Harriet began urgently, but his lordship's long, slender fingers were still clinging so tightly to her sleeve that the seam of it was threatening to come apart. "And there are the de Courceys –"

"To hell with the de Courceys!" Lord Capel dealt with them summarily.

"But it will be so highly inconvenient ... So completely unconventional!"

"Fiddle-faddle!" His lordship looked up at her with blazing, appealing eyes. "I have no use for convenience or convention, if it comes to that. And you owe me so much! If you devoted a whole lifetime to me and my service you could not repay what you owe me!"

Harriet recoiled a little.

"But only a short time ago you said that I saved your life...."

"I was delirious," the Marquis replied coldly.

"Then you must be even more delirious now," looking as if she was very much alarmed. "What you are suggesting is quite – quite extraordinary! And I am not even a nurse ... I have no real knowledge of nursing, apart from the exercise of a little common sense. And your lordship requires someone to attend to you who is skilled and capable and – and –"

"Stay with me!" His lordship lifted himself on to his elbow, and the colour was receding fast from his face. "If you don't I shall burst open my wound and sink into a decline, and all that will be on your conscience, which is burdened enough already."

"But, my lord – !"

"As a matter of fact," Lord Capel continued, casting his eyes up to the ceiling as if he was appealing for a divine dispensation on her behalf, "if I had your conscience, and were a member of your unfortunate sex, I would be thinking of going into a retreat until such time as I had either expiated my crime with much prayer and fasting, or accepted as an alternative the more human and merciful way of atonement which would lead me to the care and comfort of the sick. I am inclined to feel strongly that the latter is your only worthwhile course."

"You mean the care and comfort of yourself, my lord?" Harriet enquired with a good deal of dryness.

"Ex – actly," the Marquis replied, his voice becoming so very faint that it was an indication he was about to collapse.

Fetcham, with a mixture of perplexity and concern on his face, leaned across the bed to her and spoke urgently.

"Don't agitate him, miss. We're going to have a bad enough time with him as it is. And once he takes a notion into his head he don't get rid of it easily. I think he really will burst open that wound if you won't go along with what he says, and he can't afford to lose no more blood."

"Oh, very well." Harriet removed the pelisse she had only recently donned, and sat down again very primly beside the bed. "But it is very much against my will," she added, addressing herself to the impervious face on the nest of lace-edged pillows. "Very much against my will, and Fetcham, I hope, will bear me out on that point should it ever become necessary – should such a small matter as my reputation become involved in this quite extraordinary affair!"

"Oh, certainly." The Marquis opened one eye and smiled at her, and for the first time it struck her that he could, when he felt like it, smile in a manner which had a quite extraordinary sweetness and amiability about it – quite unlike the arrogance which settled round his mouth when he was in complete control of a situation, or the petulance reflected in his slumbrous dark eyes when he was even mildly frustrated. "Fetcham will give you his word on that, won't you, Fetcham? And do any amount of vouching for the excellence of your reputation should it become necessary!"

Fetcham mumbled awkwardly:

"If you say so, my lord. Although the young lady and I haven't met before today."

"It might surprise you to know, Fetcham," the Marquis informed him, "that until very late last night *I* hadn't met the young lady! But now that she has become indispensable to me – oh, very temporarily, shall we say? – I feel that I have known her throughout the course of several lifetimes."

Harriet merely stared straight ahead of her, as if endeavouring not to listen to ramblings such as this, and Fetcham said hastily that he would consult the landlady about the tea. And he added that if she would provide him with her address in Paddington he would set about the collection of her luggage.

"There is merely a small holdall, which is all I shall require in any case," Harriet informed him unwillingly. "And will you please inform my friend that I shall be in touch with her by letter?"

"Merely a small holdall," the Marquis murmured, echoing her, when Fetcham had left the room. "That sounds to me like a remarkably pitiful wardrobe for a young lady of so many pretensions." He was obviously becoming drowsy, and about to drift off into sleep. "It would be interesting to do something about it one of these days," his words becoming slurred.

Harriet left the bed and approached the window. What, oh, what, she asked herself, had she done to justify her involvement in such a situation as this? And then she recollected that a man was probably already dead because of her, so there certainly was a very great deal of justification.

CHAPTER
EIGHT

THE landlady brought her tray of tea and some wafer-thin slices of bread-and-butter, which Fetcham had thoughtfully ordered, and Harriet managed to accept the tray from her and keep the door only partially open so that she could see very little of what was happening in the candlelit room until she had successfully closed it again. She felt very sure the landlady would have entered the room with eyes bright with curiosity if only she had been granted the least chance to do so, but Harriet was too well aware of the dangers of the situation, apart from its unorthodox aspect, to permit her any such opportunity.

The Marquis slept for another couple of hours, and then lay awake and watched her drowsily for perhaps another hour, after which he slept again, until a clock below in the hall chimed the hour of midnight. And immediately its chimes had ceased, she heard the rumble of wheels in the street below, and a carriage drew to a halt outside.

Fetcham let himself into the house and climbed the stairs with the utmost caution. It was hardly likely that the landlady, or any member of her family, would be about at that hour, but nevertheless the manservant entered the room with a finger to his lips, and Harriet understood immediately that they were to leave at once. But she cast a glance at the somnolent figure in the bed and experienced a purely feminine reaction. He was sleeping so peacefully, and in the candlelight his thick black eyelashes lay on his cheeks in such a manner that an illusion of such complete helplessness was somehow created despite the length of his limbs and her heart contracted because they had to disturb him.

"*Must* we?" she asked. "Would it not be better to wait until morning? Or, at least, for a few more hours?"

But Fetcham shook his head.

"No, miss. That woman down below ain't in no wise to be trusted, and we've got to be gone. Apart from which, Cap'n Markham wouldn't want to be involved in this sort of thing, and, as his lordship agreed with me, the sooner we get down to Hollowthorne the better. There we can lie low until the smoke blows over, as you might say."

"Very well."

Between them they aroused the Marquis, and between them they got his cloak wrapped round his shoulders, his curly-brimmed beaver hat set well down over his shapely dark eyebrows, and his hessian boots drawn on. The Marquis groaned as they moved him unavoidably from time to time, and protested at last that he could dress himself. But due to the quantity of blood he had lost he was ridiculously weak, and his efforts merely threatened to delay them. Harriet cast a glance somewhat wildly round the room, and espying the brandy bottle and the glass beside it fetched him a fortifying but not particularly generous dose of the fiery spirit. He sent her a grateful look.

"Thank you," he said. "And now I'll have another!"

Harriet glanced quickly at Fetcham, and he nodded.

"It won't hurt him," he said. "We'd better take the bottle along with us."

It was as well that they did, for by the time they had got the Marquis down the stairs and out of the house and into a corner of the carriage which was waiting for them, Lord Capel was threatening to faint dead away. In fact, he was unconscious as they drove away, and recovered to find himself lying with his head in Harriet's lap and Fetcham regarding him uneasily from the gloom of the opposite seat.

Bright moonlight was pouring into the carriage, and the Marquis's face was so white that there was one moment when Harriet was almost convinced that that proud and arrogant spirit of his had already deserted his handsome and completely limp body. But when she called his name sharply – and she could never afterwards completely understand why she called him "Richard" – he opened his eyes and smiled up at her languidly, and apologised for leaning all his weight against her.

"If you'll give me a heave into my corner I'll be all right," he said. And then he asked with faint interest: "Where are we?"

"Crossing Wimbledon Common, my lord."

The Marquis smiled peculiarly.

"If I were a Catholic I'd cross myself," he said. "I expected to leave this place in fine fettle this morning, instead of which I'm being virtually smuggled out of the country."

"Not out of the country, my lord," Harriet contradicted him. "Only to Hollowthorne, where you can recover your strength."

"And where my brother Bruce will ask a damn fool lot of questions, and preach at me if he thinks it necessary – there was talk of his embracing Holy Orders before he went into the Army and got mowed down at Waterloo. You'll find he walks with a limp that will never allow him back into the Army."

"I'm so sorry," Harriet said.

"Oh, you don't need to be sorry! He's had his fill of the battlefield, and will probably end up hurling admonitions from the pulpit."

"Is he married?" Harriet asked.

"Lord, no!" He glanced at her quickly, and in a faintly speculative manner. "Come to think of it, you and he would deal famously together! You've both got that 'holier than thou' air occasionally, and you're both devilish determined when the mood takes you. And although he ain't much of a woman-chaser, I do seem to recollect he likes red hair."

"My hair is not red," Harriet protested, not because it really mattered very much just then, but because in her opinion it was no more than the truth. And it was not the first time he had made reference to her carroty curls. "It is a shade I prefer to describe as chestnut."

The Marquis laughed outright, which proved he was feeling slightly better.

"Women!" he exclaimed. "How full of conceit they are! Even you, who could be mistaken for a daughter of the vicarage if we didn't know you were the devil's daughter! But at least you can't deny that your eyes are as green as a cat's."

"It depends upon the particular breed of cat," Harriet replied with a good deal of stiffness. "I have known cats with eyes that were certainly not green, and even on one occasion blue."

The Marquis smiled at her good-humouredly, and Fetcham, who considered his master was talking too much, urged him to remain as still as he could and not make unnecessary inroads on his strength. The valet's eyes were forever on the moonlit road over which they were travelling, and Harriet at last sensed that it was because he was apprehensive of highwaymen. Normally the Marquis never travelled without an armed escort, but on this occasion it had been impossible to arrange for such an escort at short notice, owing to the necessity for absolute secrecy. Knowing that the coachman on the box was elderly, Fetcham was decidedly uneasy. But Harriet, unaccustomed to such a luxurious form of travel, found the smart pace at which they progressed curiously exhilarating, in spite of her anxiety for the Marquis.

The road wound like a ribbon beneath the stars, at one moment shut in by towering groves of trees, the next bathed in brightest moonlight with gorse bushes growing beside the way lifting their pale flowers to the width of the sky. There was very little that moved apart from themselves, for the birds were all nesting under the eaves of sleeping cottages, or in shrouded hedgerows, and in silent meadows there was only the play of light and shadow. Water gleamed, and dusky thickets held strange menaces ... And occasionally a light flickered under a sloping roof. A church clock showed up palely against the luminous night behind it.

One of the carriage windows was partially open, and the scent of cool grass came in. Harriet inhaled it with a feeling of great pleasure, thinking strange thoughts concerning the circumstances under which she was travelling – she who had never travelled like this by night in the whole of her life before.

What a contrast it was with the ordered routine of Lowthan Hall, with the problems connected with Verbena's limited wardrobe, with Robert's return to Oxford, with Cook's arguments with the butcher. A wounded Marquis was lying against the fat squabs of an extremely luxurious carriage, a silver-mounted pistol in a velvet-lined holster very close to his hand, undoubtedly there in case the valet's uneasiness should prove to be justified and a gentleman of the road should put his head in at the lowered window. But even the thought of anything like that happening didn't seriously disturb Harriet. She decided that she was beyond being disturbed by minor happenings of that sort, particularly as she was unencumbered by anything in the least valuable, and she very much doubted whether even the Marquis had more than a few guineas in his purse, since his preparations for this journey had been of the very slightest. Fetcham, it was true, might have made more careful preparations, but a great deal had been expected of him in a short time and it was doubtful.

Nevertheless, Fetcham was anxious. In between watching his master's face his eyes returned constantly to the road, a pale ribbon over which the horses raced while the coachman on the box exhorted them to greater efforts as he understood it was virtually a matter of life and death. But Harriet, after such a day, and with the Marquis's blood still staining her gown, was grateful for such a miraculously smooth and apparently effortless means of travel.

Fetcham had hoped they would find it unnecessary to break their journey for a change of horses, but in the early hours, with Lord Capel in a somewhat peculiar state between sleep and unconsciousness, he decided that they had no alternative but to come to rest in the yard of a little tucked-away inn. The coachman hammered on the door while the manservant descended and prepared to enter into necessary discussion when the landlord made his appearance, and Harriet bent over the Marquis. He looked up at her in a glazed way, and she explained to him gently that they had decided they must, if it could be arranged, allow him to rest at the inn. He was in no condition to continue the journey, and it was only when this seemed to penetrate to his intelligence that he uttered a husky but violent protest.

"Hell and damnation, no! We must proceed! We cannot be far away...."

But the valet returned to the carriage with the landlord in tow, and as Fetcham was plainly not in any mood to argue with his master, and that master had not the strength to resist, they lifted him between them – with the help also of the coachman – out of the carriage and into the diminutive inn parlour.

Candlelight flickered; the landlord's wife, in a voluminous nightgown, with her hair escaping from a cap that had slipped sideways on her head and was hanging down her back, got down on her knees in front of the cold hearth and re-kindled a satisfying blaze, and his lordship was ensconced in the corner of a hard settle while a bed was prepared for him upstairs. More brandy was brought – a very excellent French brandy on which no dues had ever been paid, and which the Marquis would have appreciated very much if he had been capable of appreciating anything just then – and Harriet stood by to make certain he did not fall off the settle on to the hard floor of the parlour if overcome by weakness. She had made the discovery that his wound had opened up afresh, with the loss of a great deal more blood, and from the blueness of his lips he was in very dire straits indeed.

She whispered urgently to Fetcham that a physician must be fetched. Fetcham agreed immediately and said that he would see to it that someone from the inn was sent to fetch one. Then the landlord's wife, attired somewhat sketchily in more normal garments, appeared and announced that the room upstairs was ready, and the awkward little procession upstairs began. Harriet, who followed behind automatically, found herself addressed by the landlord, who hung back for the purpose, as "my lady", and assured that the noble lord, her husband, would receive nothing but the most excessive attentiveness in his humble hostelry, and that she herself could be provided with a bed in a corner of the room if she decided that it would be better for the invalid to occupy the main bed alone, since he was in such a delicate condition.

Harriet said "Oh, no!", in hasty and horrified accents; but a diversion was created, which she afterwards lamented, when the Marquis had actually been deposited upon the bed and he refused absolutely to allow anyone to undress him. He insisted that they leave him alone and allow him to sink into a kind of semi-drunk, semi-exhausted sleep. Not even Fetcham could prevail upon him to give ground in this matter, so Harriet was allowed to place a distinctly rough blanket over him to ensure that he did not take cold, and while the others withdrew she sat beside the bed in anticipation of meeting the doctor and offering him as likely an explanation of what had occurred as she could think up in her present condition of numb weariness.

She had no doubt that Fetcham felt the need to refresh himself in the downstairs parlour, and she did not blame him. But for the first time it struck her that this was a situation which was likely to get alarmingly out of hand if she did not exercise the utmost discretion and caution in dealing with it. Her own part in the whole sorry affair was reprehensible enough, but as Verbena de Courcey's governess she had to take extreme care that her reputation as a young unmarried woman was not in any way "blown upon", as she felt certain the Marquis himself would have phrased it. And already the landlord of the inn had addressed her as "my lady", because she had not been sufficiently alert, either mentally or physically, to correct such a misconception the instant she crossed the inn threshold.

She should have corrected him at once, of course. But she had not done so. She was not entirely certain in her own mind why she had not stated in her own clear voice, and most emphatically, that she was Miss Harriet Yorke, and that she was merely accompanying the Marquis.... Accompanying a wounded Marquis, in the middle of the night, and with no tittle of reason for doing so apart from the fact that she herself was responsible for his condition; and apart from everything else between them they had succeeded in depriving another man of his life...?

Her head drooped, and by the time the doctor arrived, dragged unwillingly from his bed, but decidedly curious despite his many protestations, she had fallen so fast alseep that no one could wake her. Between them the landlord's wife and a little maidservant attached to the inn got her on to a pallet bed in a corner of the room, but were quite unable to remove her clothes because of a complete lack of co-operation on her part.

This was something to feel profoundly thankful for when she awakened the following morning and discovered that the room was full of brilliant sunshine and the Marquis was lying watching her from the pillows of a vast four-poster bed, the curtains of which had not been drawn. The Marquis's face was wan, and the expression in his eyes was perplexed, but he conjured up a slightly twisted and decidedly amused smile as he recognised how complete was the horror which overtook her as she struggled up on her pallet and realised that they appeared to have passed the night – or what little had remained of it – in the same room.

"I trust you are feeling more refreshed?" the Marquis enquired, his smile broadening as she put up her hands to her disordered hair and sought to do something about it. "You have the happy facility for sleeping like a baby when life becomes too much for you, and I'm afraid that yesterday was altogether too much for you!"

Harriet struggled to her feet and tottered to the side of his bed.

"And you, my lord?" she asked. "How are you?"

"Very much as you would expect after being dealt with by some local doctor. I gather that the fool actually bled me – what do you think of that?"

"Oh, no!" she exclaimed.

"With the result that I am as weak as a kitten. But it does seem that my fever has abated slightly."

Mechanically she placed a hand on his forehead, and was relieved because it was no longer hot and dry to her touch.

"It does seem that you are better, my lord," she told him. "That is to say, a little better . . . But I should have spoken with the doctor. I fully intended to do so."

"Instead of which you fell asleep. And now the landlord and his wife have both decided that you are my wife, and your pitifully small amount of baggage has been brought up here and you are expected to wash and dress in this room. You cannot possibly object, because there is no other room available –"

"But there must be!" she gasped. "I must have a room of my own!"

"That, I'm afraid, is quite out of the question. This is a very tiny, a very remote, inn, and mine host and his good woman have put themselves to considerable trouble to allow us the use of this room. I suspect that it is their own, and they are probably encamped somewhere up among the rafters."

"Then I, too, can be encamped among the rafters. I cannot possibly wash and dress in this room with you, my lord!"

"Poppycock!" he exclaimed, as she examined her blood-stained dress with horror. "If you imagine I shall take an excessive amount of interest in your ablutions – and, by the way, that can with the coarse towel over it contains hot water, or did an hour or so ago! – then you must be very simple, Miss Yorke, for not even the most beauteous damsel with the most delightful and engaging curves could arouse my interest at the moment. I am in a bodily state which puts such pleasures entirely out of court. Besides, there are curtains which we can pull if you will lend me your assistance."

But, afraid lest he should do himself some damage by raising himself on his pillows, she hastened forward and insisted on pulling the curtains herself. She allowed herself to show some gratitude for his consideration, and added that she would be as speedy as she knew how.

"Take your time," he advised, his voice muffled by the curtains. "I have no pressing engagements this morning, as you should be well aware. The doctor has advised that I lie here for at least another few hours, and that is what I intend to do. After that we go on – to Hollowthorne."

"But would it not be wiser if you remained here for another night at the very least?" she suggested, when she had hurriedly washed in the almost ice-cold water, and extracted a dress from her valise which, although plain, was at least free from blood-stains and of a quite a pleasing shade of blue. When he saw her, with her neatly combed hair and a delicate colour in her cheeks which had been whipped into them by the sheer frenzy of her dressing, he actually nodded his head in a sort of approval.

"I made some reference just now to beauteous females, Miss

Yorke, but I should have added that you are near enough to being a beauty yourself," he told her. He sniffed the air as if something pleasing had attracted his attention, and then demanded to know what perfume it was she used that was floating most beguilingly in the atmosphere. "It is as if a combination of roses and violets had determined to make a most brazen attack on my senses," he remarked, his eyes twinkling a little alarmingly as he lay regarding her. "Nothing from Paris, I'm prepared to wager, but some homespun concoction of your own very likely which is just as deadly."

Harriet flushed delicately but quite noticeably.

"It is nothing but toilet-water, my lord," she protested. "A distillation of lavender flowers which is not in the least deadly and which I use constantly."

"Which is one reason why I know immediately when you enter a room." He raised a finger and beckoned. "Come here!" he ordered.

But Harriet refused to move from the spot where she was standing.

The Marquis sighed.

"I am not a patient man," he told her, "and I am also a sick one, which should at least arouse your pity. Come closer that I may inhale the delicacy of your lavender-water."

"Have you had breakfast, my lord?" Harriet asked a little hurriedly, still declining to obey him.

"Something revoltingly like a very thin gruel was brought to me about an hour ago," he replied. "And Fetcham has instructions to procure me a bottle of the landlord's brandy – that will put more heart into me than anything else."

"On the contrary, my lord, it will do nothing of the kind. Yesterday you had far too much of that sort of thing, but today I shall see to it that you are fed with hot soup and nourishing beverages of that sort – "

To her horror his hand reached out and she was caught by

the sleeve and dragged close to the bed and within inches of his coarse pillow. He displayed a quite surprising strength as he partly raised himself on his pillow and drew her determinedly downwards until a lock of her hair became dislodged from its pins and fell across his face, and he laughed strangely as he buried his mouth in the little hollow at the base of her throat where her prim white fichu fell away from it.

"Tantalizing little wretch!" he exclaimed, while his eager lips explored the warmth of her throat. "Don't you know that by defying me you do yourself no good? You merely encourage a – a kind of devil in me!"

"You – you are basely ungrateful, my lord!" she protested, as she fought furiously to extricate herself from his hold. "I have devoted myself for many hours to the task of looking after you, and in return you treat me as if I were a – were a woman of no account!"

"A pretty jade, perhaps, but not of no account!" He laughed again, a trifle unnaturally, and as she saw the wild glint in his dark eyes she wondered whether he was suffering from a raging temperature, and whether, if she could reach the bell rope which had been improvised she ought to tug at it hard. And in any case his determination to detain her must be shockingly bad for his recent wound.

"Let me go, my lord!" she implored. "You will do yourself an injury – "

"You are as sweet as a whole garden of wild flowers," he told her.

"Let me go! *Please!*"

And, surprisingly, he let her go. She fell back against the wall of the tiny bedroom and he lay looking up at her sullenly, the red glow in his eyes dying slowly while a sulky look disfigured his handsome mouth.

"I apologise," he said stiffly.

The base of her creamy throat felt scorched by his wild

kisses, and she was shaking so uncontrollably that she knew he must have seen how her fingers fumbled as she sought to straighten her fichu.

"I think you must be suffering from a – from an increase of fever," she said unsteadily.

"Nothing of the sort. I am suffering from the disastrous effects of a too-pretty nurse."

"Then I will remove myself – "

"You will do nothing of the kind!" He sat bolt upright against his pillows. "Attempt to run away from me now and I will have you relentlessly pursued. That I promise you! Not until I feel capable of doing without you altogether shall you escape me. You can think me a cad – you can think me anything you please . . ."

"I do think you a cad, my lord," she assured him shakily.

His dark eyes glinted at her.

"I have apologised," he reminded her stiffly. "Do you wish me to grovel?"

"No, my lord, merely to remember that at the moment I am without status or protection as a part of your entourage, and it is not entirely through any fault of my own. If you had remembered your duty to your wards none of this would have happened."

"If you had behaved like any normal young woman it would not have happened."

"Nevertheless, it has, and – and I will go downstairs now and interview the landlady about suitable sustenance for you . . ."

"Then you had better wear this." He briskly removed a plain gold band from his little finger and handed it to her. "It was my mother's wedding-ring, and bearing in mind your unprotected state" – a cool curl to his lips – "and what even the landlord has apparently decided in connection with you, it will at least lend you a degree of respectability."

"Oh, but I couldn't!" she protested. "There is no need...."

"I assure you there is every need! Wives normally wear the badge which indicates their bondage."

"But I am not your wife!"

"Put it on," he insisted impatiently. "The third finger of your left hand in case you are unfamiliar with such things. And remember," he added, with sudden cutting coldness, "it will not entitle you to be called the Marchioness of Capel. We are unknown here."

"You mean you have given a – false name?"

"Fetcham had the common sense to do so. Now go and get yourself some breakfast, and be discreet if you are forced to converse with anyone inside the inn. Leave all the explanations to Fetcham."

"Very well, my lord," she agreed, in a very quiet voice indeed, without directing another glance in his direction, as if that would have been too painful from her point of view. And although in obedience to his request she had slipped his ring on to her finger, she removed it as soon as she was outside his room and dropped it into a pocket of her gown.

Her lips were set tightly, and she felt as if the skin at the base of her throat had been indelibly marked. To keep it company the colour flamed all over her cheek and chin and brow. Did he imagine she wished to be known as the Marchioness of Capel? Even if only for the brief time it would take them to remove themselves from the inn and reach Hollowthorne, where it would of course be unnecessary to continue such a piece of deception. Did he really and truly imagine that, even for so short a space of time, it would afford her pleasure – some sort of gratif.cation – to be thus temporarily enobled? She who had been born simple Harriet Yorke and had been so outrageously ill-used that she was shaking still from the memory of it.

To be dragged down on to his bed in such an uncouth way, and subjected to the touch of his lips!

She entered the small parlour of the inn determined that nothing of the sort should ever happen again. Despite his threat to pursue her she would leave him the moment he forgot himself again. The landlord's wife, who must have been faintly surprised by her high colour, provided her with tea and a lightly boiled egg. Afterwards she went out into the garden to look for Fetcham, with the intention of getting him to swear (on oath if necessary) that he would not provide the Marquis with any more brandy, however insistent the Marquis himself might be.

Later she returned upstairs and found Fetcham shaving the Marquis, and the two of them were discussing the advisability of an almost immediate departure from the inn. Harriet, who had no intention of spending another night under the strain of sharing a bedroom with Lord Capel, raised no objections. She agreed that as Hollowthorne was no more than twenty miles away the sooner they reached it the better. She occupied herself with gathering together the various items of their luggage that had been unpacked, and assisted Fetcham with the somewhat frustrating task of getting the invalid on to his feet.

She did not assist with his dressing – remaining outside on the landing while this was in progress – but lent the invalid the support of her shoulder (inadequate as it was) once he finally emerged. Having successfully placed his hat on his head and a cane in his hand, she supervised his descent of the narrow staircase with a good deal of care. She felt reasonably certain he could have managed perfectly well without her assistance if he had made the smallest effort, but he did not appear to wish to make any effort whatsoever. He preferred to be considered very fragile indeed.

As soon as they had entered the carriage Harriet slipped his ring back into his hand.

"Take it, my lord," she said. "I believe it is solid gold."

His shapely dark eyebrows arched a little.

"You do not even wish to keep it as a souvenir?"

"Certainly not. I cannot imagine any reason why I should wish to retain it, quite apart from the fact that I believe you said it was your mother's wedding-ring. For that reason alone it must have a great deal of sentimental value for you."

The Marquis smiled and glanced at her a little oddly out of his night-dark eyes, making use of his sweeping dark eyelashes to give the impression that he was regarding her through them.

"You are right, of course," he agreed. "No other ring could have such sentimental value for me. But it might surprise you to know that I have known women who would have been delighted to keep such a ring, had they been presented with the opportunity, as a souvenir of having known me."

"I have no doubt of it, my lord," Harriet replied. "But, as far as I am aware, you have not besought me to keep your ring, and I have no intention of ever being named amongst them!"

Fetcham, who had heard every word of this exchange, coughed, and the carriage bowled out of the inn yard.

CHAPTER
NINE

THE journey to Hollowthorne was accomplished well before dark. As the carriage turned in at a pair of gates which were leaning a little drunkenly from their stone supports, Harriet was able to make out the pleasing outlines of a house lying in a slight hollow which she recognised immediately must be centuries old.

It was approached by a somewhat neglected drive bordered by thinning elms, and more trees rose in a protective cluster behind it. Steep gable ends and twisted chimneys rose against the last of the light. The same light was reflected in numerous diamond-paned windows, and altogether the effect was extremely pleasing despite an air of neglect which spread amongst the gardens surrounding them on all sides. Unpruned roses and overgrown borders caused Harriet to utter quite a sharp protest, and Lord Capel, who had been dozing throughout the last few miles – and whom she had treated with a good deal of wariness throughout the drive, maintaining as much distance as possible between them on the seat – opened an eye in faint surprise and enquired whether anything was amiss.

"Nothing, my lord, save the condition of your grounds," Harriet replied on a note of censure, "I am astonished that they are in such very bad shape."

The Marquis glanced around him with a faint air of distaste, and admitted that he had never thought very much of Hollowthorne.

"I can't remember when I came here last," he confessed. "It

is one of those properties which my family seems to have accumulated over the years, and it was an ideal spot for Bruce to recover his strength in when he came out of the army. And now it is to be my retreat also."

Harriet was not conscious of a need to console him or to offer any soothing rejoinders, for no one had insisted that he fight a duel with Greville Aintree. She leapt from the carriage as soon as the steps were put up and stood looking about her on the drive in front of the house with her chip-straw bonnet on the back of her curls, and an expression of honest approval on her lightly flushed face.

A gentleman had emerged from the house and was standing in the porch, watching her. Harriet turned to him, and at once she knew who he was. He was so like the Marquis that it was really quite ridiculous, and yet he was plainly younger, and his hair was considerably lighter. He was wearing a dark blue coat of no very fashionable cut, although it fitted him rather well across the shoulders and drew deserving attention to the excellent way he held them; but to her horror she noticed that a sleeve was empty, and it was secured in some manner to the breast of his coat. Impulsively she stepped towards him.

"Oh, I had no idea that you had lost an arm as well!" she exclaimed. "I am so very sorry! Lord Capel said merely that you had a limp – " And then realising what she had said she apologised. "Forgive me, my lord!" A bright blush suffusing her cheeks, she went on, "You must dislike it very much when your war wounds are discussed by an absolute stranger. . . ."

"A very enchanting one, if you will allow me to say so," Lord Bruce returned, bowing formally over the hand which she offered, while a twinkle invaded his eyes. "And as for your being a stranger, well, that is soon remedied." He made an attempt to click his heels. "Lord Bruce Wendover, at your service, ma'am! Am I to be offered a certain amount of enlightenment?"

"Of course." She smiled. "I am Harriet Yorke."

"*Miss* Harriet Yorke?"

"Oh, yes, of course." The colour in her cheeks burned rosily. "Of course," she repeated.

"For the life of me," he assured her, while the twinkle in his eyes became more positively recognisable as a twinkle, "I cannot think why it is so." He cocked an eyebrow at the recumbent figure in the carriage. "That is my brother, is it not?" he asked. "Fetcham appears to be having some difficulty in inducing him to leave the carriage. Is he ill?"

"Oh, no, my lord, he is wounded!" Harriet was immediately conscience-stricken because she had deserted the side of her patient, who, she had no doubt at all, was resenting it. "He has sustained a nasty wound in his arm —"

"Don't tell me he has been fighting in somebody's war? I imagined we were enjoying a period of peace."

"It is nothing like that, my lord." She darted back to the carriage to lend some assistance to Fetcham. "He was wounded in a duel! It is because of that we have come all this way from London. Lord Capel requires to remain for a while in seclusion here!"

"Devil take me!" Lord Bruce exclaimed. "You mean he is running away from the law? Which means he despatched his man?"

"Y-yes, my lord. Although we are not yet entirely certain . . ."

"Upon my word," the Duke of Coltsfoot's younger son exclaimed in some amazement, "I have never known Rick to be as careless as that before. Either he is in love or his skill has deserted him."

The Marquis descended painfully to the gravel, and he glared with undisguised fury at his brother.

"Do you have to engage my nurse in prolonged conversation, Bruce?" he asked. "When a man has lost as much blood as I have over the past two days, and has been consumed by fever, he expects to be supported on all sides – not deprived of his main prop!"

"Very likely you are in the right of it," Lord Bruce replied good-humouredly, at the same time offering him a shoulder to lean upon; "but it certainly does strike me that Miss Yorke is a somewhat inadequate prop. There is so little of her, and there is quite a lot of you. However, if she has been engaged to attend upon you as a nurse, that is a somewhat different matter, I suppose."

The Marquis exclaimed pettishly:

"Damn it, she was not engaged to do anything at all! But why otherwise would I have brought her along with me?"

Lord Bruce shrugged.

"Your concerns have frequently, in the past, been a little obscure to me, Rick," he told him. "So you mustn't be entirely surprised if I am a trifle fogged on this occasion." He nodded at the ancient manservant who had somewhat belatedly made his appearance, and urged him to lend a hand. "Get Mrs. Rawlins to prepare a room for Lord Capel, and a room must also be prepared for Miss Yorke. I'm afraid, Miss Yorke, that you will not be very much impressed by the comforts of Hollowthorne, for they are practically non-existent, but we will do our best to ensure that you are not actually uncomfortable. Of course, if I had had the least idea that I was to expect visitors I would have made some provision beforehand."

"That is perfectly all right, my lord," Harriet assured him, as between them they manoeuvred the Marquis into the low-ceilinged sitting-room on the right of the most attractive hall, and he sank with an air of the greatest possible relief into the first available armchair. "But it is such a delightful house I'm sure I shall enjoy my very brief visit here – " she stressed, quite deliberately, the words "very brief visit", since she had no intention that it should be anything else – "very much indeed, and I do trust you will not put yourself about on my account," she added hastily.

The Marquis emerged from the trance-like state which his condition of exhaustion had temporarily induced to observe bleakly that she had no need to crawl to his brother, since the house did, after all, belong to him, the Marquis of Capel. And he added further that any expenses incurred by their visit would be borne by him.

Harriet was somewhat amazed that Lord Bruce appeared not to mind in the very least this timely reminder that he himself was permitted to reside at Hollowthorne only as the result of a charitable gesture on the part of his elder brother. And that he was not in a position to entertain regally did not appear to upset him, either. Or, rather, the inference that he was in a slightly more impecunious position than the other members of his family, despite the sacrifice he had made at Waterloo.

He limped to the sideboard and produced a decanter and glasses, and although Harriet refused refreshment the Marquis, as always, appeared to be in dire need of it. Then Fetcham appeared and announced that his master's room was ready for him, and he made the suggestion that the Marquis's arm should be looked to the instant they had got him upstairs. The Marquis agreed, and signalled to Harriet that she should accompany them upstairs, but Lord Bruce intervened.

"I hardly think that is necessary," he objected. "Miss Yorke is obviously tired after her journey, and if no more than a change of bandage is required I'm sure Fetcham can attend to it."

The Marquis protested immediately.

"But Miss Yorke is my *nurse*!"

"A highly experienced and fully qualified one?"

The Marquis swore softly.

"No, damn it, but she is my nurse all the same!"

"Then she will attend to you tomorrow morning, after

she has had a good night's rest. I'm sure you will both benefit from a night's rest after such an extraordinary experience as you both appear to have survived. In the event of an emergency I will summon our local physician."

But Harriet stood uncomfortably at the foot of the stairs, and she followed the ascent of her patient and his manservant with an anxious expression in her eyes. There was no doubt about it, Lord Capel was climbing the stairs in as laborious a manner as he knew how, but she had seen the look in his eyes when he had decided to accept his brother's dictum that she would attend to him in the morning and not argue the matter further, and it had reminded her of the faintly rebuffed, faintly hurt look of a small boy. Although he had said something pettishly about not expecting much from any woman, least of all one who owed him a debt and was not sufficiently high-minded to wish to repay it, she still thought she should have accompanied Fetcham upstairs and at least supervised the removal of his bandage.

She looked a little helplessly at Lord Bruce, who was observing her with a slight smile, and said that she thought she should have made herself as useful as possible to the Marquis. He had, after all, sustained a most unpleasant wound.

"Quite," Lord Bruce agreed, in a remarkably soft and very pleasing voice for one who in the past had been accustomed to issuing orders. "But Fetcham is perfectly capable of dealing with him tonight, and indeed I would trust Fetcham to grapple successfully with almost any emergency. Now, I suggest you go upstairs to your own room, which I believe is the small guest-room at the head of the corridor directly facing you when you reach the top of the stairs, and I will see to it that Mrs. Rawlins brings some dinner to your room on a tray."

"I could perfectly well fetch a tray from the kitchen myself –"

"Not while you are a guest in my – er," he corrected himself, "brother's house!"

She smiled at him with swift sympathy and understanding.

"I am very sure Lord Capel is delighted to have you taking care of his house for him," she told him, although afterwards she considered such a speech a trifle impertinent. "Houses such as this cannot be neglected, and, indeed, they are apt to fall into decay –"

"Which Hollowthorne commenced to do a full century and a half ago," he replied. "Unfortunately it has never seemed to have much appeal for its owners, and Rick positively objects to it on the grounds that it is hidden away and too small for his taste. For my part I find it very suited to my particular requirements at the moment. But then I am a soldier with no brilliant future ahead of me, and no very real idea what I am to make of that future – minus an arm, as you were so quick to find out! And that unfortunate anomaly, a younger son!"

"I do apologise, Lord Bruce," Harriet said uncomfortably. "It was appallingly rude of me to comment on your arm!"

"Not at all," he assured her, And she discovered that when he smiled his somewhat haggard face was transformed, and one thing that had rather puzzled her about him became finally clear. His eyes were several degrees lighter than Lord Capel's, a sort of chestnut brown, warm and reassuring and transparently honest, quite unlike the glinting darkness between the heavy fringes of the Marquis's luxurious eyelashes. "I could hardly believe my good fortune when I saw you alight from my brother's carriage. My life here is so unrelievedly dull that a visitor such as yourself is like an apparition from another world. So I beg you do not apologise to me for anything whatsoever!"

"But, Lord Bruce," she said to him earnestly, "I have to make it clear to you that my visit is quite an accident, and indeed I have to leave here very soon. Perhaps – perhaps if I could – talk to you about the quite extraordinary situation in which I find myself. . . ."

"Yes, yes," he replied to her reassuringly, "you shall talk to me tomorrow. We will have a family conference – I have a feeling that Rick is in some ridiculous form of trouble which we shall have to do something about. Almost certainly if my father is not to hear of it! Now, can I persuade you to go upstairs to your room and rest? You do badly need rest, of that I am quite assured."

Harriet was inclined to agree with him, and at the same time she wondered what he would say if he knew that she had slept for at least a part of the night before in the Marquis's own room. He had said that she need not apologise to him for anything, but she was very certain he would consider that more than a little strange. And so would a very large number of other people! Her father, most certainly, if he was alive. . . . Indeed, he'd probably insist that the Marquis married her without a moment's delay and be ready to run him through with his own small-sword if he refused!

And although the Marquis might laugh uproariously at such a notion, and particularly at the threat of the small-sword, how would he react if his sister, Lady Fanny Bingham, had been involved in such a situation . . .? Or the lady over whom he had fought a duel, despite the earnest advice of his friends!

As she mounted the stairs Harriet felt her feet dragging a little, for she was really so tired that she wondered whether she would have the strength to undress herself before crawling into bed. And if she had had to take yet another look at the Marquis's wound after so many hours devoted to travelling and quite unwonted excitement, she knew that it was more than possible that she would have actually turned faint. She was filled with gratitude for the kind intervention of Lord Bruce.

But when after following, in a spirit of meek obedience, the directions issued to her, she reached her room at last and saw the can of hot water covered by a snowy towel on the dressing-table, her bed turned down and a fire crackling in a lively manner on the hearth, her spirits revived, and her gratitude increased. Even if she was not provided with any dinner she would have little to grumble at so long as she was allowed to sleep in peace.

But dinner – an excellent dinner – was provided, and it was the housekeeper herself who conveyed it to her room. Elderly and rheumaticky like her husband, and almost overburdened with curiosity rather than resentment because she had had to bestir herself and ensure that the unexpected visitors received adequate attention, she fussed over Harriet like a hen with one chick, apparently not in the least surprised that she was a part of the Marquis's entourage. It could have been that she was accustomed to the Marquis making occasional descents on lonely Hollowthorne with one of his lady friends (not, perhaps, altogether acceptable in the circles in which he was accustomed to move!); but Harriet preferred to think that this was not so. She preferred to think that Mrs. Rawlins was a naturally kindly woman with an amazing facility for creating feather-light dumplings, who enjoyed looking after exhausted young women like herself, and making absolutely certain that the hot brick in their bed was well wrapped up in layers of flannel, and that the supply of fuel beside the hearth was not likely to be seriously diminished during the hours of darkness should she find it impossible to sleep.

Fortunately for Harriet she slept soundly, and in the morning she awakened to find her room full of sunshine and the fire still smouldering on the hearth. When she leaned from her window to take a good look at the morning she was charmed by the trailing scarves of mist that had already ascended high among the branches of the trees and were rapidly evaporating in the warmth of the sun, and by the blue of the sky that hung like a canopy above Hollowthorne. And although on the previous afternoon she had thought the grounds overgrown, she now considered them delightful. The air was piercingly sweet with the perfume of the sprawling roses and with the perfume of wallflowers and violets and early lilies and jasmine, delicate tendrils of which climbed right up to her window inviting her to detach a small sprig for her own adornment, which she sniffed with acute pleasure as she made her way downstairs for breakfast.

Mrs. Rawlins had informed her that breakfast was served in a room known as the Oak Parlour, and having discovered it, and also made the discovery that Lord Bruce was there before her, she entered it a trifle shyly.

Lord Bruce rose at once, and greeted her with enthusiasm. She had put on a sprigged gown, and her curls were shining; her complexion was like the pale heart of a pink china rose, and her eyes were as clear as a trout stream. When she smiled, as she did a little uncertainly, her lips curved upwards engagingly at the corners, and dimples lurked at both sides of her mouth. Lord Bruce's brown eyes beamed at her, and he thought of sunlit meadows and little streams and uncurling buds of springtime blossoms.

"Good morning, Miss Yorke," he greeted her. "I do trust you slept very well?"

"Oh, excellently," she replied. "Excellently!"

He carved her a slice of delicious pink ham which was on a side table, and placed a basket of newly baked bread close to her elbow. In response to his ring Mrs. Rawlins brought her a tray of tea all to herself, the enormous silver teapot striking her as a little absurd, but very welcome nonetheless. When she got to the stage of sampling Mrs. Rawlins' own preserve she declared that she had never tasted anything quite like it before. The Marquis of Capel was very fortunate in having such an excellent pair of servants left in charge of Hollowthorne, and before she left she simply must persuade the housekeeper to part with one or two of her recipes which she could take back with her to Lowthan Hall when she returned to it.

"Lowthan Hall?" Lord Bruce looked decidedly curious at her mention of it. "Where is that? Am I to take it that that is where you live? If so, it is a very fortunate place indeed!"

Blushing slightly, Harriet explained that it was where she earned her living as companion to the two youngest de Courceys. That statement would have involved her in an immediate explanation of the somewhat curious situation in which she found herself, had she not already made up her mind that she would say nothing of any particular relevance until she had had an opportunity of seeing the Marquis. He was on her conscience, and she was simply not in the mood to dwell upon other matters for the time being, she explained carefully. As soon as she had finished her breakfast, she thought she ought to go upstairs and look at her patient, if only to prevent him running another high temperature as a result of fancied neglect.

"So if your lordship will excuse me . . .?" as she rose.

Lord Bruce, who had just dissected a particularly rosy apple and removed its core, looked up at her with a slight frown.

"But surely," he objected, "there is no very great urgency? I looked in on him myself early this morning and he appeared to be sleeping quite peacefully. And Fetcham, I am sure, would have acquainted me with any deterioration in his condition."

"Nevertheless, I think I ought to ascertain for myself that all is well."

"You take your duties very seriously?"

"They are not precisely my duties, my lord." She looked down demurely at the skirt of her gown. "It is rather a matter of my conscience, as Lord Capel pointed out to me on our arrival here yesterday. You must have overheard him say something of the kind."

"Rick has a habit of making statements with which I could in no wise agree," Lord Bruce told her, looking, however, a little curious as he did so. He eyed the shapely but very capable-looking hands smoothing the front of her dress, and then glanced upwards at her lowered white eyelids and her faintly drooping mouth, with a wry twist to its corners. "At least, not on every occasion. You must not allow him to affect your judgement in matters of any importance to you, Miss Yorke ... And certainly you must not allow him to make unreasonable demands of you!"

"No, my lord." But her small smile remained inscrutable, and her long eyelashes did not lift. "And now, if you will excuse me, my lord –?"

"But of course," he said, and rose and stood watching her as she left the room, the apple he had prepared for her remaining on his own plate, while her light feet carried her swiftly upstairs.

She tapped cautiously on Lord Capel's door, and Fetcham called to her immediately to come in. His lordship was already up and dressed, which considerably astonished her. He was sitting beside his window. His expression was noticeably dour, but although he was interestingly pale and there were dark shadows under his eyes as if he had suffered a good deal, and was still suffering to a certain extent, there was no doubt that he was already on the road to what might yet prove to be a slow recovery.

"Good morning, my lord," she said, as she moved into the middle of the room. "Is this not early in the day for you to be out of your bed?"

The Marquis glared at her.

"If it is, then there is no reason why you, at least, should comment on it," he replied. "Your attitude since we arrived at Hollowthorne has made it abundantly plain that my progress, whether uphill or down, is not of the slightest interest to you. I trust," he added formally, "that you slept well? I have no idea where they put you, but from your appearance you were provided with a reasonably comfortable bed."

"Oh, I was, my lord," she assured him. "A very comfortable bed! Your housekeeper, Mrs. Rawlins, is a very kind woman, and she looked after me so well that I feel a new being. And I have just breakfasted in the company of your brother. I find him very pleasant, too."

"Excellent," Lord Capel growled. He indicated a chair facing him. "Sit down. You and I have a good deal to talk about, and it is long overdue."

"I fail to understand how you arrive at that conclusion," she told him in a gentle voice, as she ignored his invitation and decided to risk resting a hand lightly on the coolness of his forehead. He refrained from taking advantage of the gesture. "Splendid!" she exclaimed. "You have no fever."

"I am perfectly well aware of that."

"And as for any conversation between us being long overdue, we have only known one another for a matter of two days and nights. Admittedly, it does seem to be rather longer than that."

"You know very well that I am referring to the conditions under which we have known one another. It is seldom, I imagine, that a young woman of your years and station finds it necessary to share a bedroom with a man about whom she knows little or nothing, and is compromised to such an extent that the landlord of an inn assumes she is a married lady and refers to her as such. And as I am the author of these tribulations of yours, Miss Yorke, I'm dev'lish concerned about the position – and dev'lish disturbed!"

"Why, my lord?" She sat down obediently facing him – Fetcham having discreetly left the room – and confronted him with a smooth, and utterly unreadable, creamily-pink face lighted by those water-green eyes of hers. She fluttered her eyelashes a little, and looked down at her hands. "What is so very disturbing about my position?"

"I've just said that you've been damned well compromised!"

"But only in a very remote and tucked-away inn, which we are neither of us very likely to see again." For an instant her eyes met his, and she was intrigued by the curiously baffled expression in the lustrous dark depths surveying her. "And for most of the time Fetcham was with us. I'm sure he constituted an excellent chaperon, apart from the one occasion when – when –"

"Ah, there you have it, girl!" He nodded his head at her in some satisfaction. "Apart from the one occasion when I dragged you down on to the bed and behaved towards you in a highly reprehensible manner! Fetcham was not there then! And even if he had been I doubt whether you would have gained much support from him! Why, dammit, don't you understand . . .? He is used to – to –"

"Ladies of a slightly different persuasion whom you entertain from time to time?" Harriet suggested softly.

Lord Capel swore.

"If I do, it's nothing whatsoever to do with you, you impertinent chit. Why in heaven's name I couldn't think of some way of ridding myself of you for good and all when you came to me that night in St. James's Square I can't think," he lamented helplessly. "Believe me, I would have done so if I could! I never at any time liked the look of you, with those great green eyes of yours, and that critical expression which is the most uncomfortable thing about you! You sought to make me feel a villain, and you even accused me of annexing the de Courcey brats' fortune. . . ."

"No, no," she replied. "I merely sought to remind you of your duties."

"Well, now it is all one and the same thing! You have got me holed up here like a fox, and I have no knowledge of what is happening in London. For all either of us know to the contrary Aintree is already dead, and both Markham and Cavendish are implicated. My father will be in a state of mind beyond description, and my sister Fanny hardly able to put her head out of doors –"

"And for all of this you blame me, my lord?" she asked him quietly.

"I do! Oh, yes, I do! You have become a kind of a – a blight, an evil influence. . . ."

"And what of the lady over whom you fought the duel?" she asked him, in a quieter voice still, while her hands clasped one another very tightly in her lap. "Does she not bear some sort of responsibility for all that has happened to you?"

"What, Melissa? Good lord, no! She is a – a woman of the town, a little more refined than most, perhaps – a beauty! Certainly, when I look at you I regard her as a quite outstanding beauty –"

"Thank you, my lord," she said, with tightly compressed lips.

He looked momentarily ashamed of himself.

"I apologise," he said. "I am behaving quite outrageously and it is certainly not my intention to affront you. You have looked after me very well indeed, and as a matter of fact I regard you as an extraordinarily good nurse. I am by no means certain what I would have done without you after that – that debacle at Wimbledon."

"I am sure you would have managed very well indeed, my lord," she told him with a certain irony.

"That is where you are wrong," he assured her. "Somehow or other you impressed me with the extraordinary strength of character which you have, and I actually felt inclined to lean on you – to clutch at you like a straw!"

"A foolish thing to do when the straw is an evil influence," she observed unsmilingly.

"I only said that because I – I am in a bad mood this morning! Oh, hell!" he exclaimed, resting his head in his hands for a moment. "Hell and damnation! Why am I going on like this when I have something else to say? Before my brother can get at you! Before anyone else can get at you!"

Harriet felt herself stiffening on her chair. Like an animal scenting danger she scented an outrage to her pride.

"What is it, my lord, that you have to say to me?" she asked very quietly indeed.

He raised his head and looked at her. There was reproach, and bewilderment, and even a kind of appeal in his eyes.

"Why, dammit, what is there I can say to you except one thing? Are you so utterly unworldly that you don't expect it! Are not prepared for it?"

"I give you my word, my lord," she replied to him, "that even if it means confessing I am excessively unworldly, and therefore probably a little stupid, I have no idea at all what it is you have to say to me." As this was not entirely true she hoped the lie would be forgiven her. "No idea at all.'

"Then you must indeed be very stupid." He glared at her, shook his head because he realised he was behaving clumsily if not contemptibly, and then satisfied his honour by bringing out the request bluntly. "Will you marry me, Harriet? Damn it, you'll have to marry me!" he added, "Especially after the way I behaved to you this morning!"

Harriet rose from her chair very slowly and composedly and walked over to the window. Looking out at the sunlit brilliance of the garden she strove to concentrate on one aspect of it, a bed of wallflowers in the midst of which a graceful stone figure was silhouetted against a dark box hedge behind it.

"I wouldn't marry you, my lord," she told him, considering the appealing outlines of the figure, and the surprising way in which the box hedge had been kept carefully clipped, "if there was no other man in the world from whom it was in the least likely I would receive a proposal of marriage. At the moment I can in all truthfulness assure you that there is no other man, and it is very likely I shall end my days as a most embittered spinster, concerned with the well-being of young people like the de Courceys, and attending to the wounds of gentlemen like yourself who get themselves injured for no practical reason whatever. But even if it meant confinement within the walls of a convent as an alternative to marrying you I would not marry you ... And now I think, perhaps, I had better look at your arm and satisfy myself that it is completely healthy!"

CHAPTER
TEN

Two days later, at an hour when the sun was sinking most pleasingly behind the avenue of elms and the mellow red bricks of Hollowthorne were glowing like rosy apples in the last of the light, Harriet found herself walking in the garden and feeling no small degree of astonishment, as she inhaled the perfume of the borders, that she was still an occupant of the house and still in some sort of attendance on the Marquis of Capel.

She had talked to his brother, Lord Bruce Wendover, and discussed her position in some detail with him. Only an hour or so earlier they had sat among the roses and examined the situation with a good deal of earnestness. Lord Bruce was of the opinion that Harriet had been shamefully used, and he did not even consider she merited reproof of any kind for having taken it upon herself to affect the outcome of the duel between his brother and Greville Aintree. On the contrary, he seemed to think her action indicated extraordinary presence of mind – which Harriet herself disagreed with completely, since she knew only too well that she had been motivated by blind and quite unreasoning panic. She had wanted to see neither of the two men involved despatched by the other, and she had behaved as she would have behaved under a number of similar sets of circumstances. For instance, if the young de Courceys had been taking an airing in their governess-cart and the horse had bolted she would have darted out unhesitatingly into the road to stop it had she seen it approaching.

But the case of Lord Capel and Mr. Aintree was a very different matter. Lord Capel had been wounded and Mr. Aintree was probably already dead ... And it was all due to her and her over-hasty reactions.

But Lord Bruce shook his head very firmly.

"I cannot possibly agree with you," he said. "If you had not interfered my brother might very well be dead, as he himself seems to believe. And as for Aintree, well, we have no knowledge as yet that he is dead."

"But the surgeon very plainly entertained little hope of saving him."

"All the same, confirmation of his death is one thing, and the fear that he might die is quite another. And as for Richard ... well, he had no business to be fighting a duel in the first instance! And if what you say about his wards is true, then he had certainly no business to be fighting a duel while no provision whatsover had been made for them and their future. And this is something I cannot understand. How did he come to be the accepted guardian of such a bevy of young things? It is quite unbelievable to me!"

"Robert is old enough to attend the university, but the other two are quite young," Harriet admitted. "But in any case Lord Capel denies that he accepted the guardianship willingly – or even that he accepted it at all. Which makes the whole thing seem very strange indeed."

"It seems devilish strange to me," Lord Bruce agreed. "It is so unlike Richard to take on such a charge, when I've never known him dote on anything younger than an opera singer in the female line, or a frequenter of Cribb's Parlour in the male. However," looking somewhat embarrassed as if afraid that his observation had been in rather poor taste, she having little or nothing in common with an opera singer of the order his words conjured up, "it is possible he was under some sort of an obligation ... but I cannot imagine how that came about. Richard is exceptionally cautious about becoming involved in anything in the least likely to recoil on him."

Harriet found it easy to believe that. The Marquis's proposal of marriage had been made because his conscience had dictated it, but it had been perfectly clear to her that his fears of the trapdoor closing on him had depressed his spirits to such an extent that, had anyone other than herself been involved, she might have been a little sorry for him.

Fortunately for him she had put him out of his misery with no delay whatsoever.

She said suddenly, and with faint curiosity in her tone:

"It would have been different, of course, if Lord Capel had been a trifle older, or if he had been married! A married man, with the support of a wife, would have been better able to cope with a set of completely strange wards. Although on the other hand his wife might raise objections, and will very likely do so when – when Lord Capel does eventually marry!"

At the back of her mind was the thought that, at some time or other in his life, judging him to be somewhere in the region of thirty, or perhaps thirty-two or three years of age, a suitable wife for Lord Capel must at least have been thought of, and perhaps strongly proposed, by some member of his family. Lady Fanny, for instance, was hardly likely to have been completely inactive when it came to the selection of a future sister-in-law.

Lord Bruce shrugged.

"When Richard does marry he will no doubt surprise us all, but it has long been understood – or perhaps I should say hoped for, since I am convinced he has done nothing positive about it – that the Lady Rowena Harmsworth will become his affianced bride and the future Marchioness of Capel so soon as he becomes aware that it is incumbent upon him to marry, and that a man in his position cannot evade such an issue indefinitely. She is the daughter of the Earl of Headcorn and a great beauty, and they have known one another for years."

"I see," Harriet murmured.

"But of course," Lord Bruce continued, "the situation could become a little delicate if and when Richard explains to her that he has already acquired a certain amount of responsibility in the shape of these de Courcey children. And naturally, if he is to marry, he will have to make a clean breast of the situation."

"Naturally," Harriet agreed.

Lord Bruce glanced at her. His eyebrows drew together a little.

"But it is you who are causing me a great deal of concern, Miss Yorke," he told her. "Through no fault of your own you have become involved in the most unpleasant aftermath of an exceedingly rash piece of behaviour on my brother's part, and I do not quite know how to advise you. You could return without any further delay to Lowthan Hall and the young de Courceys, but as we have no real knowledge of the condition of the unfortunate Aintree I hardly think that is the wisest thing – having due regard to all the circumstances and, in particular, Richard's predicament – you could do. Your own interests would undoubtedly be well served if you hesitated no longer and left Hollowthorne tomorrow morning, but Richard's would not. If Aintree is dead then arrangements must be made for him to leave the country, and it is important that no one apart from ourselves and his closest friends should have the least idea where he is hiding at the present time. I know he dislikes very much the thought that he is forced to hide away here, and I believe that if it were not for my father he would not care very much for his own safety and wellbeing. But my father does have to be considered, and you do see that anyone who could provide clues to Richard's whereabouts, and who could be questioned –?"

"By the law officers, you mean?" Harriet said.

"Well, yes ... There is no doubt about it, the Runners will be on to him if Aintree dies and possibly he is already dead. In which case they will be looking for him already, and since it will have become known that you have spent some time in his company –"

Harriet smiled wryly.

"I do seem to have become involved, don't I?"

"But I do beg of you don't let it worry you!" Lord Bruce laid a hand gently over one of hers, where it rested in her lap. "On no account must you worry too much about your own involvement in this sorry affair! When I said that it will become known that you have spent some time in my brother's company, what I actually meant was that the purpose of your visit to him in London will have become known, and naturally it will excite a certain amount of curiosity. But whatever happens I will personally see to it that you do not come out of this with even the slightest shadow on your reputation! I give you my word on that!"

Harriet thanked him, but she was a little at a loss to understand how he could prevent her reputation from becoming sullied if the full story of the events of the last few days ever became known and provided a titbit for gossip in many aristocractic homes throughout the country – to say nothing of the London clubs. And at the thought of her own impetuosity and stupidity she felt herself squirming a little.

Lord Bruce gave her hand another squeeze.

"Promise me you won't worry your head about all this," he said.

Harriet smiled at him a little blankly.

"I promise you, my lord, that I shall never find it easy to forgive myself for the outrageous way in which I consider

I have behaved," she replied. "Lord Capel would be far better off than he is at this moment if I had stayed quietly at Lowthan Hall and continued to bombard him with my letters. At least they were comparatively harmless, and growing a little tired of receiving so many he might one day have replied to them."

Lord Bruce shook his head.

"Richard is the one who is at fault. Richard betrayed a trust."

"But the odd thing about his betrayal," Harriet informed him, "is that I am entirely convinced that he was never at any time aware that he was acting in a reprehensible manner. Which does seem to indicate that he was the victim of a rather serious error."

"I will have the whole matter out with him," Lord Bruce promised, and then recollected that he had various duties to perform within the house, and begged her to excuse him.

Left alone, Harriet commenced to pace about the garden, until in the fading light her concentration was rudely shattered by a disturbance on the other side of the hedge beside her, which overlooked the main highway skirting the property. A vehicle was approaching along this narrow country road, to the accompaniment of a rattle of carriage wheels and the thud of horses' hooves; and as Harriet peered through a gap in the hedge she caught a glimpse of a particularly smart equipage which passed within a couple of feet of her, and a minute or so later turned in at the drive gates and started to proceed towards the house.

Harriet felt an urge to remain well hidden in her tucked-away corner of the grounds, but curiosity overcame her after a short while and she made her way cautiously back to the house by means of some little used and overgrown paths, in time to see the carriage making its way between the sentinel-like elm trees, and finally coming to rest before the entrance porch of the house. A groom leapt from his horse and the carriage steps were let down; a door emblazoned with a coat of arms was flung open, and on to the ill-kept sweep before the front door descended Lady Fanny Bingham, the upstanding feathers on her modish hat dipping and swaying eccentrically with every slightest movement she made, her gloved hands fluttering dramatically and her silken skirts swirling about her.

Harriet recognised her immediately, and without the smallest difficulty. For although she had only seen her on one previous occasion her likeness to her brother, the Marquis, was almost absurd, and she had precisely the same air as the Marquis as she stood looking up at the closed door of the house and plainly regarded the fact that it had not opened to her immediately as a justifiable cause for impatience. She called sharply to her groom to attack the knocker afresh, and when at last Rawlins opened the door a very few inches she upbraided him in no uncertain terms for keeping her waiting on the doorstep.

"Upon my word, Rawlins," she remonstrated, "I was beginning to be certain you were all dead! Indeed, I was positively convinced of it! What in the world were you about, behaving as if the house was under attack and an enemy likely to gain entrance?" More sharply still she demanded: "Where is my brother? Where is Lord Bruce?"

Lord Bruce made it unnecessary for the butler to so much as attempt a reply by limping out on to the doorstep. If he felt any pleasure at the sight of his sister he managed to conceal it admirably; but his greeting was polite and courteous enough.

"Why, Fanny! My dear Fanny, what brings you here? Don't tell me there is bad news of Papa?" with a sudden show of anxiety. "His health is not as good as usual –?"

"No, no." Fanny waved at him a hand encased in lilac kid. "Nothing in the least like that. To the best of my knowledge

Papa is in excellent health, apart from his gout. But I have a piece of the most upsetting news to impart to you which has brought me all the way from London without pausing for a single change of horses. I am utterly exhausted and I have never been more concerned in my life. Pray stand aside from the doorway and allow me to collapse into the nearest chair. . . ."

Lord Bruce moved hastily aside, and his sister entered the ancient hallway with a further swirl of her skirts and a mad disturbance of the feathers on her hat. Harriet, who had hidden temporarily in the shrubbery close to the house, approached the front door steps with a good deal of caution and timidity, and was just in time to overhear Lady Fanny's high-pitched, hysterical revelation of the extent of the disaster that had befallen the family before the parlour door closed and further revelations were confined to the inside of the oak-lined parlour.

But Harriet had heard enough to have a certain amount of sympathy with Lady Fanny. Apparently the very worst thing that could possibly happen, to the Marquis of Capel at any rate, had happened. Greville Aintree was dead, and Lady Fanny had it on the very best authority.

Harriet was so deeply shocked and disturbed that she hardly knew what to do for a full five minutes after the information had reached her ears. Lord Capel would be gravely upset, she knew, and as for herself – she felt the very next best thing to a murderess.

She stood there in the silence of the hall, actually wringing her hands, and wondered what in the world she could do if the rest of her life was to be in the least supportable. To deprive a man of his life! It was such a very dreadful thing to have happened, and the most dreadful thing about it was that the knowledge would haunt her all her days, and there was nothing she could do about it – nothing at all! – that could wipe out her guilt or alter the situation in the very least.

She was a murderess! No matter how many excuses might be made for her, no matter how desperately she might seek to excuse herself, Greville Aintree was dead, and she and Lord Capel between them were responsible for his death.

She had no idea how long she remained there in the hall, consumed with an anguish she had never expected to experience, before the parlour door opened and Lord Bruce came out. Shocked by the sight of her white face and staring eyes, he realised at once that she had heard the news, and he put an arm very gently but firmly about her shoulders and drew her into the parlour.

Lady Fanny was lying almost full length upon a settee, fanning herself with her hat and sipping a glass of Madeira with relish after her journey, and standing in front of the fireplace, beautifully dressed for the evening, was Lord Capel himself. Apart from being a little pale, and holding one arm a trifle stiffly, there was nothing about him to indicate that he had recently been very much an invalid. And apart from a strange, rather feverish glitter in his eyes, there was no sign that he was disturbed by the news his sister had brought him.

"Ah, so there you are, Miss Yorke!" Lady Fanny exclaimed, smiling brightly upon her, while Lord Bruce hastened to put a glass of Madeira into her hand. "I had no idea I would meet you here, but it is really most fortunate because I have something to tell you about those charges of yours. Knowing how concerned you were for them and their welfare I journeyed deep into Sussex to visit them and see for myself how they were faring, and you can accept it from me that there is now very little amiss with them, and Verbena is coming to stay with me in the near future. Robert has gone back to Oxford and the little boy, Ferdinand, is living happily at the vicarage with his tutor. Of course we shall have to consider their whole situation seriously very soon, but for the moment all is comparatively well and you have nothing at all to worry about. Does that not set your mind at rest?"

"Oh, yes – yes, indeed, ma'am," Harriet replied, feeling so little concern for the members of the de Courcey family at that particular moment that she found it quite impossible to sound in the slightest degree enthusiastic.

Across the width of the room she met the Marquis's eyes, and although they did not smile it struck her that they seemed cynically amused. He lifted his glass high in the air and suggested they drink a toast to the de Courceys.

"At least that problem appears to be solved, at any rate temporarily," he said. "Which is fortunate for them, since I shall have little opportunity to supervise their well-being while I am roaming the Continent during the next two years. What about you, Miss Yorke? You look a little pale at the moment. Is it because there is a thought at the back of your mind that you might be forced to share my banishment with me?"

His sister rebuked him for being unnecessarily facetious; and she added further that she considered Miss Yorke's part in this very unfortunate affair to be so very trifling that no one need consider it further. She had acted as any young female of sensibility might have acted under such circumstances, and the fact that she had risked her reputation somewhat needlessly by consenting to act the part of a temporary nurse to her brother was in itself commendable, if one overlooked the fact that she had displayed a disregard for the conventions.

"But then I understand your father was away at sea a great deal," she concluded, directing at Harriet a rather more censorious look than she had hitherto done, and allowing a strong note of censure to enter her voice; "and no doubt your mother was beset by so many problems that the bringing up of a daughter along lines which everyone could approve was no simple matter for her. However, I am a little surprised that you should have been quite so reckless. Capel has a reputation with members of our sex which is hardly likely to reflect credit on you should the story of your close association over the past few days ever become a subject for public gossip. I'm sure you understand that and are as concerned about the situation as I am?"

The whiteness of Harriet's cheeks was suddenly stung with painful colour, but she denied emphatically that either her mother or her father had ever failed in their duty where she was concerned. On the contrary, they had been exemplary parents. . . .

"It is I who occasionally behave with – with an impetuosity which no one can deplore more than I do myself," she admitted very stiffly, finding difficulty in controlling a tendency on the part of her lower lip to quiver a little.

Lord Bruce bent over her and patted her shoulder almost paternally.

"There, there, Miss Yorke," he said, "forget it, I entreat you. All this is most unfortunate, but you are by no means to blame."

Lady Fanny waved a hand at her carelessly and, somewhat surprisingly, agreed with her younger brother.

"Of course you are not to blame, but should such a situation ever arise again I trust you will think not merely twice but a great many times before behaving, as you yourself admit you occasionally behave, with impetuosity." She wagged an admonitory finger at the Marquis. "And as for you, Richard . . . What Papa will say about this, and what will be the effect on his health, I shudder to think. As a family we shall none of us escape criticism –" although when she thought about it afterwards Harriet found it difficult to follow her reasoning on this head. "I personally shall go into seclusion for a while until the storm blows over."

"In heaven's name why?" Lord Capel demanded, in an irritated way. A certain whiteness at the corners of his mouth indicated that he was experiencing a reaction to the shock of the news of Greville Aintree's death, and Harriet at least sensed that he was stunned by it. Somewhat to her own surprise she felt a profound sympathy for him. "I have heard of the sins of the fathers being visited upon the children, but never of the failings of an elder son being visited on his entire family."

"But that is precisely what happens when an elder son forgets his duty to his father, and his *obligations* to every other member of his family," Lady Fanny told him, waving her wine-glass above her head as an indication that she desired it to be refilled. Lord Bruce obligingly carried the decanter over to her settee. "And now, my dears, I propose that we forget our problems for a short while and enjoy our dinner. I am almost ravenously hungry, and I understand that Mrs. Rawlins has received instructions to prepare a suitable meal for us, and no doubt my maid has already unpacked for me upstairs." She rose gracefully from the settee. "I shall not bother to change into anything very elaborate, but I certainly must rid myself of these travel-stained garments. Now, Bruce, at what hour do we dine?"

"Normally at this hour we would already have dined," Lord Bruce admitted, wondering whether the strain upon the resources in the kitchen would prove too much for Mrs. Rawlins, and what, if anything, would be provided for dinner. "But since Hollowthorne has suddenly become as popular as a coaching-inn," with a certain amount of dryness, "I trust you will overlook a certain amount of confusion on the part of the servants and make allowances if the repast which they are likely to give you is a trifle inadequate as well as late." He did not look as if he altogether welcomed the advent of his fashionable sister, particularly after the last two pleasant evenings when he and Miss Yorke had dined alone together, but as the duties of host more or less devolved upon him he was plainly prepared to make every endeavour to rise to the occasion. He looked a little regretfully at Harriet, as if she was rather more in his mind than the other two, and it was to her rather than the others that he addressed himself before he bowed himself out. "If you will forgive me," he said, "I will pay a visit to the kitchen and discover whether any difficulties have arisen which I can deal with satisfactorily."

Lady Fanny watched his departure with a certain amount of interest – indeed, quite a lively degree of interest. And no sooner had the door closed upon him than she turned and looked directly at Harriet and arched her eyebrows in a particularly meaningful way.

"Well, well!" she exclaimed. "Well, well! Who would have thought it? – Of Bruce!"

She smiled with sudden dazzling brilliance at Harriet, collected her reticule and her gloves and her enormous milk-maid hat with the brilliant feathers attached to it and the satin ribbons which looped beneath the chin, and moved in a wave of excessively expensive French perfume to the door. Once she reached it she paused and blew a light-hearted kiss at the Marquis.

"Never fear, Rick," she encouraged him. "All will yet work out! And one can be so very gay in Paris, and indeed in Venice also – although I must admit that dreadful stench from the canals is a little distressing." Another thought occurred to her and she sobered still more. "And it is really most un-fortunate that Rowena Harmsworth returned from Italy only last week. She confessed to me that she was looking forward very much to seeing you again, and her mama was so very eager to hear how you did. I had the feeling they were both listening intently for the sound of wedding-bells!"

Richard made no response whatsoever, and gazed unsmilingly

at his sister. As soon as she had closed the door he walked to the window.

Harriet rose at once and said something about lending some assistance in the kitchen also, but his lordship turned and walked swiftly towards her. Surprising her considerably, he put out both his hands and possessed himself of hers, and held them very tightly.

"I'm sorry, Harriet," he said. "I'm so sorry that I find it difficult to express myself."

Harriet gazed up at him uncomprehendingly.

"You mean," she faltered, "that you are sorry about – about –"

"Not about Greville Aintree. Oh, I'm sorry that the surgeon failed to save him, of course, but he was not a pleasant man – you, certainly, would not have thought so! – and he had sent so many others to their deaths. No; I am sorry because you look so utterly downcast. You were plainly distressed when you came in here a short time ago! But you must not blame yourself, Harriet – it was *not* your fault! You acted humanely! It was my fault for calling him out!"

"You – you said he might have killed you . . ." Harriet faltered – wondering why the clasp of his hands was such a comfort to her in those moments.

"I certainly think he intended to do so. But," with harsh dryness, "would that have been such a very great loss to the civilised world?"

"Oh, yes! Oh, indeed, yes!" Looking up at him with her limpid green eyes she recognised, not for the first time, how exceptionally handsome he was; and with that despondent droop to the corners of his mouth and the melancholy in his eyes he had become all at once a far more insidious threat to the normal tranquillity of her mind than she would ever have believed possible; certainly not in her moments of unswerving common sense. "Oh, yes, my lord," she assured him with a notable degree of emphasis.

He smiled, and there was a tinge of the old mockery in his smile.

"Answer me something truthfully, Harriet," he requested her. "Would you have agreed so unhesitatingly had that question been put to you on the night we met? Would you?"

Harriet looked downwards at their clasped hands.

"I – I – " she attempted, but failed altogether to pursue the matter.

He laughed softly.

"Oh, fie, Harriet," he said, and put his fingers under her chin and lifted it, looking directly into the green eyes. "What has brought about this change of heart? Not the difficult invalid I have so recently proved, for he must have affected you sorely at times with the temptation to abandon me altogether. But you did not do so! You were remarkably true to your trust, and I find it quite astonishing ... particularly as you have since refused to marry me. That was an experience quite novel to me."

"I'm sure it was, my lord," she replied with a sudden tightening of her lips.

He shook his head at her.

"Pray remember that I *did* ask you to marry me, and that is something I have never done before. I have never placed myself in such a vulnerable position before."

"But you must have been very certain that I would refuse you, my lord. You could never for one moment have supposed that I would accept you."

"Couldn't I?" He frowned a little as he regarded her, and he was still holding one of her hands. "But you and I have experienced an extraordinary intimacy, Harriet, and our situation is unique – or that is how I regard it. If you had had the least regard for your own reputation you would have accepted me without a moment's hesitation, and I – I might well have had cause to be grateful to you. You are not as most women of my acquaintance are, or sooner or later become. You are neither afraid of me nor enamoured of me, and you have discovered a method of handling me which is astonishing. When I consider how physically inadequate you are and how deprived of a suitable background, I marvel that you should have had so little hesitation in championing the cause of those wards of mine, for one thing."

"It was my duty," she told him, seeking to avoid his eyes. "And when it is a woman's duty she cannot allow herself to be affected by any considerations of weakness."

"And therefore, as my sister has it, you bearded the lion in his den – apparently on her recommendation! – and here we are. And the problem now is – in my new life, so far away from all tender reminders of home and friends, how am I to forget all about you?"

"I am sure you will manage very successfully, my lord," she told him drily, although for the first time since she had known him she wished almost ardently that he did not arouse in her such a desire to be antagonistic.

"I'm afraid I cannot agree with you."

"But as Lady Fanny observed such a short while ago, Paris – and Venice! – can be remarkably gay. And the Earl of Headcorn's beautiful daughter may well decide that England has few charms if you are not to be numbered among them, and consider another trip to the Continent much more to her taste if she is likely to encounter you there. Consider, my lord, how your exile could be rendered less irksome and your loneliness less oppressive if the two of you should meet in one of those faraway capitals. It is not impossible to contract a marriage on the Continent, I believe."

She glanced at him swiftly and then looked away again.

"So you think I will be lonely?" he said broodingly, ignoring the rest that she had said.

Harriet shook her head.

"Not really, my lord. I was forgetting that you must have many friends in Europe."

"Even if I have, there are bound to be occasions when I will think of England – and you! Yes, you, Harriet! I would like you to know that I will think of you very often, and it will not be to my comfort."

He carried both her hands up to his face and held them there for several seconds before kissing them. Harriet's face flamed, and the most extraordinary reaction took place deep at the very centre of her being. She felt as if her whole inner being trembled a little, and from the nerve centres in her fingertips to those located in the region of her heart a most disturbing message was despatched.

She hastily snatched away her hands, and said that she must go and lend Mrs. Rawlins some assistance in the kitchen. It was really too much for the poor woman to have to cope with all the problems of providing a meal of several courses for so many people, and it was up to her to lend a hand.

"I really must go ... If you will forgive me, my lord?" she said.

And before his reply that he would not forgive her and that he had much more to talk to her about could fall on her ears, she had opened the door and departed. Lord Capel stood looking after her with a frown between his brows.

CHAPTER
ELEVEN

THE dinner, when it was brought to table, was a tribute to Mrs. Rawlins' capacity for rising to the occasion despite a poorly stocked larder, and Lady Fanny was loud in her praise of the hastily plucked and roasted chickens; and in particular the fruit tart seemed to her to merit unstinted approval. She had attired herself in the palest blue gauze, and her head-dress was a spectacular achievement on the part of her maid, who had found the restrictions imposed upon her by a somewhat limited supply of candles a little difficult to overcome.

Nevertheless, Lady Fanny was happily conscious of appearing at her best, and as a result was in high good humour. Harriet, who had had no opportunity to make any alteration to her appearance owing to the fact that she had been assisting Mrs. Rawlins in the kitchen until just before the dinner bell rang in the hall, felt slightly overawed every time her eye, either by accident or a kind of hypnotised design, lighted upon her.

And as for the Marquis, already dressed for the evening before his sister arrived, in dark blue velvet coat and white satin small-clothes and silk stockings, which would have been entirely appropriate for either White's or Crockford's, let alone a tucked-away Elizabethan manor house, seemed to her to lend him so much dark and devastating distinction that the contrast afforded by his brother Bruce was a little unfair.

Lord Bruce was most decidedly eclipsed by his two close relations, having none of their striking good looks, although pleasant enough to look at. And the uniform he had worn at Waterloo was decidedly the worse for wear despite Rawlins' efforts to deprive it of its many stains and blemishes.

However, as a more pleasing contrast with his brother, whose mood was once more glum and unapproachable, Lord Bruce was an urbane and an attentive host, and in the drawing-room after dinner – the dust-covers having been removed and a fire kindled on the hearth – he persuaded Harriet to play the piano for them, and she obligingly recollected some country dances and other pieces which were applauded languidly by Lady Fanny, reclining once more on a settee, and not applauded at all by Lord Capel, seated in some isolation at the far end of the room. Lord Bruce displayed so much enthusiasm that Harriet, who considered her own talents in this direction to be limited, was a trifle embarrassed, and when the tea was brought in she was only too happy to take over the task of dispensing it and thus prevented Lady Fanny disturbing herself on her settee and bringing on a condition of exhaustion which she seemed to dread. As she explained at some length, exhaustion was the one thing she always strove to avoid, since as a result of it she might quite possibly be laid low; and after such a day devoted to travelling as she had endured solely on her brother's behalf she could not be too careful.

Her brother Bruce agreed with her that Sussex roads were becoming impossible, but once again Lord Capel said nothing. He did, however, firmly decline to partake of any tea, and while the others were sitting comfortably over theirs walked to a window in an alcove and stood staring out into the night.

Just before nine o'clock Lady Fanny started to yawn ostentatiously, and declared that she was for bed. Harriet jumped up immediately and offered to accompany her upstairs, alarmed no doubt by the prospect of exhaustion overtaking the Duke's daughter on the way to her room, but Fanny smiled at her sweetly and said that her maid would be waiting up for her and she was perfectly capable of mounting the stairs without assistance from anyone.

"Stay and play backgammon with Bruce," she urged, smiling almost knowingly at Bruce. "He tells me you are such an expert he was quite unable to defeat you when he played with you last night. How is it you have become such a deadly opponent, Miss Yorke?"

"My father insisted that I play all parlour games as well as he did himself," Harriet replied.

"Indeed?" Lady Fanny strove hard to smother a yawn. "Then my father, His Grace of Coltsfoot, will delight in playing chess with you at some time when the two of you have become acquainted. Pray remember that that is an obligation I have laid upon you."

She waved a hand airily to the room at large, wished them goodnight and tottered towards the door. But when Lord Bruce prepared to set up a table for backgammon Harriet said hastily that she would prefer to withdraw to her own room, too, and Lord Bruce's expression of acute disappointment made her feel most uncomfortable as she prepared to climb the stairs. She wished she had not made such a favourable impression on him, for he was a lonely man, and when she departed he would be more than ever aware of his own loneliness, and that was not a fitting reward for a veteran of Waterloo. Surely Lady Fanny could have found him a suitable wife if only she had made the smallest effort?

Before she reached the head of the stairs Harriet caught the sound of voices, and she realised that the two men she had left behind in the drawing-room – one of whom had not even wished her goodnight – were already talking to one another. She wondered whether they were discussing plans for the Marquis's highly necessary departure from his own country.

Breakfast was scarcely over in the breakfast-parlour the following morning when a clattering of hooves on the drive interrupted the peaceful consumption of tea and coffee and freshly-made toast, and sent Lady Fanny to the window to discover who it was who had arrived. She had already astonished everyone by putting in an appearance at such an early hour, when her normal custom was to lie abed until nearly noon; and now, apparently, she was in such a state of agitation to get pressing matters over and dealt with, leaving her free to return to London, that her first thought was in connection with her brother, and her immediate fear was that a bevy of Bow Street Runners had already scented him out and had arrived to achieve his arrest.

But with a gasp of relief when she peered from one of the open lattices she recognised the ducal emblem on the near-side door of the glistening carriage drawn up at the foot of the front door steps. A very elderly gentleman was being assisted to alight by a tall young man in a many-caped coat and curly-brimmed beaver hat, and while Harriet, who was beside her at the window, recognised the tall young man as Charles Cavendish, Lady Fanny plainly recognised a very much more personal connection.

"It is Papa!" she whispered. "Now, what in the world – *what in the world* – has brought him here at this most awkward moment?"

"Very likely he has come to say goodbye to your brother," Harriet replied, because that was the only explanation that occurred to her.

"If that is so it will cause him a heart attack, for Richard is the light of his eyes, the successor to his Dukedom, and his one reason for continuing to live."

Although Harriet found it a little difficult to reconcile a desire to live with the probability of sustaining a heart attack she murmured sympathetically. Lady Fanny clasped her hands in agitation and declared that it was all quite unfair.

"You haven't the least idea what it is like to possess a father who dotes on only one member of his family," she lamented, "and that member quite unworthy. If Richard was a little more considerate I might find it easier to forgive him, but as it is I hold it strongly against him. And now I have to deal with my papa!"

She left the window and crossed the room so swiftly that she was in the middle of the hall waiting to receive him with open arms when the Duke crossed the threshold and stood looking about him with a certain amount of distaste. He glanced upwards at the cobwebbed rafters and then downwards at the unpolished floor boards, and the expression on his face became increasingly dubious. Being very tall and still fairly upright for his years he had to bend his head to avoid cracking it against a beam; and beside him Charles Cavendish, who had lent him the support of his arm, had to do precisely the same thing, while out of the tail of his eye he caught sight of Harriet only just emerging from the doorway to the breakfast-parlour.

Instantly his whole expression registered the utmost approval.

"Your servant, ma'am," he said, as soon as he had released the Duke into the charge of his daughter. "I never expected to find you here!"

"And I certainly never expected to find myself here," Harriet replied, colouring in some confusion because the occasion of their last meeting had been attended by some exceedingly unorthodox circumstances.

Fanny was embracing her father in the middle of the hall and chiding him at the same time for making such a taxing journey, which in point of fact was no more than a matter of forty miles or so, over the border into Hampshire. But when he replied testily that he had a right to do precisely as he pleased, and if his son was going into exile then it was only a normal and natural thing that he should wish to extend to him his blessing which he could take with him, and which might provide him with some solace during the years of his exile, she simply shook her head at him and assisted him into the breakfast-parlour. There he allowed himself to be lowered into a chair at the head of the table, declared that he had already breakfasted, and announced that in any case his son wasn't going into exile, because the damned fellow he shot at was going to live after all.

"What!" Fanny exclaimed, and everyone listened and held their breaths because it seemed very likely their ears had deceived them.

The Duke of Coltsfoot lay back in his chair and smiled in a highly gratified and satisfied manner.

"It's true," he insisted. "Devil take me, it's perfectly true, and the best piece of news I've had to impart in a lifetime. Charles here will support me, for it was he who dropped all his engagements and rode hell-for-leather into Hampshire to break the news to me as speedily as possible. I've told him I can never show enough gratitude to him, and the two of us set off for this benighted spot which seems to me to have fewer charms every time I come to it. But if Bruce doesn't mind living here, and it doesn't drive him to distraction, then he can have it for all I care – and for all, I'd be prepared to wager, Richard cares!"

"Yes, Father," Fanny agreed impatiently. "But what of Greville Aintree?"

"Sitting up in bed and astounding his doctors because he's taken on a new lease of life, or so it seems. All that bad blood he lost must have done him more good than half-a-dozen leeches."

"But we were assured that he was dead – "

The Duke waved an impatient hand.

"Poppycock! Fellow can't be dead and alive at the same time, can he? And I tell you he's very much alive! Ask Cavendish over there, he'll tell you there ain't no doubt about it."

Lord Bruce and Charles Cavendish were entering into an earnest conversation just inside the doorway, and Harriet could tell by their expressions that they were both experiencing an inordinate amount of relief. Harriet herself could hardly believe what she had just heard . . . For it meant that she was no longer a murderess. She had not, after all, killed a man, or been in any way responsible for his death, and the relief in her case was so tremendous that she had to put out a hand and grasp at the back of a chair for support.

The Duke of Coltsfoot, having broken his news and been exceedingly gratified by the response, decided that after all he could enjoy a second breakfast, and Lord Bruce carved him a plateful of ham and cold mutton, and made a descent into the wine-cellar to search amongst the empty bins for a bottle of something which might possibly have been overlooked during the past few days when Hollowthorne was forced to entertain the Marquis, and which his Grace could be expected to describe as "tolerable". And while he was conducting his search the duke recollected the most urgent reason for his visit, and demanded to know where Lord Capel was hiding himself.

"Damn it, there's no danger from the law now that the whole thing is over," he declared, "and I won't even read him a lecture if he gives me his word that he'll never engage in anything so foolhardly again. I forgive him freely," he assured his daughter, "and that's remarkably generous when he might have been the death of me. My doctor has issued so many warnings on the condition of my heart that you're all well aware that I have to be treated gently, and Capel has a duty to consider me above everything else. Which makes his conduct all the more reprehensible, and naturally I have been deeply pained."

"I'm sure you have, Papa," Lady Fanny said soothingly.

A thought occurred to the Duke, and he looked suddenly anxious.

"Charles said something about the boy receiving a scratch, but it wasn't anything worse than a scratch, was it? He's all right? He's not lying upstairs in a serious condition? Dying, perhaps – !"

"No, no, Papa, he's all but completely recovered."

"Then why hasn't someone told him that I'm here? Why is he taking such an unconscionable time remembering his duty and letting me see for myself that he's all in one piece? Devil take it, he's my heir! I'm fond of the boy – "

"Which is extra ordinarily generous of you, your grace, when I've done so little to deserve your affection," the Marquis observed from behind his chair. "And I owe you many apologies for causing you so much concern."

Harriet, who had not so far been introduced to the latest distinguished visitor, withdrew discreetly as father and son clasped hands and regarded one another in a manner that showed how strong was the bond of affection between them, and Lady Fanny followed her from the room. She slipped a hand into Harriet's arm and guided her towards the garden door as they crossed the hall, and as they emerged into the soft brilliance of the morning and the flower-scented atmosphere her ladyship confessed that she had wanted to have a word with her, for they had many things to discuss

"Now that my father is here and that wretched Aintree is to live after all we must begin to make plans," she said. "There is no longer any nightmare hanging over us to cause Richard's departure for the Continent, for it is fairly certain he will return with my father to Coltsfoot, and I shall suggest to him that after a short filial stay he opens up Capel. The house is one of the most beautiful in the country and simply ideal for house-parties on the grand scale, and with Lady Rowena Harmsworth returned to this country it is more or less incumbent upon him that he involves himself in a great deal of entertaining."

She glanced quickly sideways at Harriet, as if to ascertain that she not only had her complete attention but that she understood fully the implications in what she had just said.

"Lady Rowena is almost unbelievably beautiful, and it has always been my dearest wish that she will one day become my sister-in-law. I'm sure you appreciate how very happy I now am that this might very soon become possible."

"Oh, yes, indeed, my lady," Harriet murmured, without revealing either by tone or expression that she was not in the most fervent agreement with her. It was true that she kept her eyes downcast, but as she could have been admiring the borders that was easily understandable.

Lady Fanny gave her arm a little friendly squeeze.

"Then there is Bruce ... Not my favourite brother, but so very worthy. And he did suffer so very dreadfully during that terrible engagement at Waterloo – indeed, I sometimes think that it has altered him completely. But no doubt with time and under the happiest possible circumstances he will regain a little of his old delight in living. He was never precisely enamoured of our sex, but he has everything to commend him in the marriage stakes. Naturally, should he marry, his financial position will have to be secured in some way, but that will be up to my father."

Harriet remained silent, and Lady Fanny continued:

"And now we come to you, my dear Miss Yorke ... you who have done so much for Richard that you actually endangered your own reputation a little unwisely. However, so few people know about this that I'm sure it will do you no real harm, and in any case I have so many plans for you that you have nothing to worry about. I suggest that you return with me to London when I leave here tomorrow, and Verbena can join us in a short while. I had the notion of accommodating you both in the old schoolroom in my house, but it is now in use as a bedroom and would afford you very cramped quarters since the whole house is very small. But all that can be resolved when we have settled the little boy's future, and made certain that Robert is to stay at Oxford."

"Then it is your intention that Lowthan Hall should remain closed, ma'am?" Harriet suggested, feeling suddenly that everything had got out of hand, and it was all the result of her impetuous journey to London. "That will mean dismissing the servants, will it not?"

"Oh, no, my dear, nothing as unpleasant as that, since I'm sure that most of them have been employed at the house for a considerable time. And in any case Sir Robert will take over there as soon as he is of age, and there will be the question of somewhere to spend his vacations. In the meantime my brother will administer the estate, or his lawyers will attend to it, and I give you my word there will be no difficulties over finance or anything of that sort. In the past it was unfortunate that Capel did neglect his duties in this matter, but since it has been pointed out to him – and *I* have done my share, I assure you, to convince him how badly he has erred (quite unintentionally, I give you my word) – that the pass to which his negligence reduced the de Courceys was highly reprehensible, he is determined it shall not occur again. He has been very much shocked and concerned to learn the true facts, and is under an obligation to you, my dear, because you took such a positive step to bring the matter to his notice."

Harriet supposed the step she had taken had been very positive, as well as highly unconventional, but since her knowledge of the Marquis was now very much greater than it had been when she set out from Sussex she was not prepared to accept that he was "very much shocked and concerned". It was likely that he had an unpleasantly guilty feeling, but that was as much remorse as she was prepared to allow him.

"I'm sure Sir Willoughby, if he was alive, would be very grateful to you, ma'am," she said quietly.

Lady Fanny betrayed a sudden desire to ally herself with her brother in this matter by exclaiming pettishly:

"That wretched man! Why on earth he had to burden

Richard with his brood of children I cannot think. It was entirely due, I am convinced, to some profound mistake in the very beginning."

"Have you made any effort to find out from the Marquis himself why he accepted such a charge?" Harriet enquired.

Lady Fanny regarded her pityingly.

"My dear girl, of course I have, but his explanations are a little vague, and I suspect that it was his good nature that was imposed upon. He really is extraordinarily good-natured and generous, you know, when he is not in one of his more difficult moods. And fortunately if he marries Lady Rowena she will know precisely how to handle him, and it is unlikely he will make any similar mistakes. My only fear is that she will not take at all kindly to the acquisition of three unknown wards, one of them still very much a child ... *That* may present a problem which could be a little difficult to overcome."

Charles Cavendish was coming along the path towards them, and Lady Fanny hailed him with some relief, disliking the thought of major problems ahead, but confident that she had settled the problem of Harriet with a good deal of subtlety and finesse. And if all her plans worked out there would be cause for rejoicing in the family, and one member of it at least would have cause to be grateful to her.

The Duke decided to remain for at least one night at Hollowthorne, and as there was a scarcity of suitable bed-chambers Harriet willingly gave up hers to his grace in exchange for a very much smaller room into which she personally carried her own belongings. She also assisted Mrs. Rawlins with the making up of the bed for his grace, and lent further assistance in the kitchen. Later in the day she was presented to the somewhat autocratic old gentleman who immediately mistook her for a housemaid, having come upon her while she was smothing the coverlet on his bed and settling the lace-edged pillows; and when Lady Fanny, who effected the introduction, said very clearly that she was a young friend of her own the Duke of Coltsfoot seemed immeasurably relieved because, as he afterwards confided to Charles Cavendish, she was a "damned pretty little piece", and he wouldn't have to chase her round the kitchen table if he wanted a word with her.

When he learned that her father had served under Nelson with a considerable amount of distinction he wanted to have more than a mere word with her, and invited her to sit beside him in the drawing-room after dinner and recount as many episodes about her father as she could recall. Afterwards, when he learned she played chess, he was highly delighted, and she was not allowed to take part in any other activity throughout the whole course of the evening until, with a few skilful moves, he had succeeded in beating her.

Harriet, who had allowed him to beat her, being in fact a superior player owing to her father's instruction, was aware that the Marquis of Capel came and leaned on the back of her chair from time to time and watched the game, but the Duke waved him away.

"Be off, my boy! I know she's as pretty as a picture, and I understand she's devilish good at looking after the sick, but she's uncannily good at moving these pieces about the board, and unless I keep my weather eye well open I'm going to be beaten fairly and squarely. Now, run away, Capel, and talk to your sister. No doubt she'd like to hear the full story of your recent exploits, even if they don't cover you in very much glory."

The Marquis wandered away, and Harriet wondered how she was going to continue to concentrate on the game. She and Lady Fanny were leaving Hollowthorne very early in the morning, and it was unlikely that she and Richard Wendover would find any further opportunity to discuss their exploits of the past few days. She had sensed that the Marquis wished very badly to talk to her, but he did not dare to override his father, and when he was dismissed he flung out of the room and there came the sound of an outer door closing.

Harriet thought of him wandering the flower-bordered paths in the light of a risen moon looking so shatteringly handsome. And she thought of the Earl of Headcorn's beautiful daughter driving in some state into Hampshire to be a guest at Capel, and as a result she made an unwise move which brought forth a little chuckle of delight from his grace.

"Now, now," he cautioned, "not so impetuous, m'dear! That was a damned silly thing to do!"

And a few seconds later she had surrendered her bishop, and a few seconds later still the game was his.

Lady Fanny was seated at the piano and demonstrating the high degree of talent she possessed, with Charles Cavendish bending over her and turning the sheets of music for her, when Harriet left the room, and a lively polonaise followed her as she climbed the stairs to her new little room which was no more than an attic room under the eaves. By the time she reached the gallery, which was a chequerboard of light and shadow – crystal clear moonlight and infinitely black shadow – the music was a faint and faraway echo, and since she had neglected to collect her candle from the hall table she had to grope her way forward in somewhat unfamiliar surroundings. A tall shadow appearing suddenly before her very nearly startled her out of her wits, manifesting itself as it did out of one of the denser patches of sable gloom, and only the Marquis's voice prevented her from uttering a cry of alarm.

"Oh, brave heart!" Lord Capel said mockingly. "To have ventured as far as this with never a light to show you the way!"

"I forgot to collect my candle," Harriet explained quietly,

and stood still in front of him, aware that he was watching her with exceedingly bright and lustrous eyes.

"Did you intend to leave here in the morning without wishing me farewell?" he asked her.

"I – I supposed I might have an opportunity to say goodbye to you before we left," she answered.

"But I am not, as you know, an early riser, and I understand my sister wishes to be away before the cocks start to crow."

"She – she does wish to make an early start, yes."

"Then we had better say our farewells while there is no one on hand to witness the tender nature of them, don't you agree?"

"I – do trust your lordship will make a complete recovery very soon," she responded somewhat hurriedly, and then realised that he had moved until he was within a foot or so of the spot where she herself was standing.

"And that is all? After such a short but intimate acquaintance is there nothing more than that that you have to say to me?"

"Only that – I shall do my best to look after Verbena, my lord, and to fall in with the plans your sister is making for her. I understand there will be no problems in future in connection with her upkeep."

"Financial problems, you mean? Oh, no," carelessly, "I shall release whatever monies are needed for her support, and for the support of the two boys. And naturally I shall pay you your salary, which is almost certainly in serious arrears. You need only to apply to her for whatever is required whenever it is required."

"Thank you, my lord," she murmured, and thought that the lustrous eyes surveying her developed a positive glint of mockery.

"As my father has it, you are as pretty as a picture, my dear, and as you are also a highly capable nurse I feel that some encouragement should be offered to you, and certainly some reward, and I would like you to purchase on my behalf some small present which might appeal to you as soon as you reach London. My sister will advise you, and naturally she will receive instructions to pay for whatever it is. You must look upon it as a token of my deep appreciation for all that you have done for me – and believe me, I consider you did a good deal!"

Harriet felt herself stiffening a little at the barely veiled insolence of his tone, and she half turned away as if she would leave him without further ado, but although she did not actually see him move she realised that he had successfully prevented her from escaping along the gallery as she had planned.

"Don't be in so much obvious haste to leave me, Harriet," he protested. "After tonight you and I may not see each other again for a very long time. As you are probably aware, I have various duties to perform, both as my father's eldest son and a prospective bridegroom! If you think of me at all, you must think of me dancing attendance on the so-beautiful Lady Rowena ... And, believe me, there are few women in England who can hold a candle to her! She is quite ravishing, and almost unbelievably accomplished. My sister is of the opinion that Capel is a most appropriate background for her, and I am inclined to agree with her. Capel sadly needs a mistress who will shine like a jewel in a setting which must have been specially designed for her. At least, that is how I look upon it ... Fate is so clever at arranging these matters, don't you agree?"

Harriet remained silent.

The Marquis sighed suddenly.

"But you have ministered to me so very tenderly, Harriet, that I shall miss you very much indeed. I am by no means certain Lady Rowena will have the same facility for watching over me as you have done. However, in life there is always something to regret, is there not?"

As Harriet continued to remain silent he sighed again.

"You have no conversation tonight, Harriet, and that is a pity since we have to part. But remember that all good – and bad – things come to an end. Tomorrow at this time I shall be far away from here, and you will be at my sister's house in London. You will not be dull, for I am fairly certain my brother Bruce plans to follow you, and perhaps one day you will take pity on him and marry him. As a family we would be very grateful to you if you did that, for he has served his country well, poor fellow, and had little reward. And think how well you would fit in here at Hollowthorne if I bestowed it on you as a present!"

She attempted to push past him, but he seized her hands and pulled her up against him with a degree of roughness which took her aback.

"Oh, no, Harriet," he said huskily, "you will not escape me before we have wished one another a suitable goodbye. Even if I am to marry Lady Rowena she will not grudge me this!"

And his arms fastened about her so tightly that she could not possibly escape, and when she attempted to avert her face his hand forced it out into the open and she felt his kisses descending on her unprotected cheeks and chin and brow – descending like rain. And then his hot lips found her mouth, and her futile efforts to keep him at bay collapsed altogether, and she was completely still in his arms. The ancient gallery with its portraits and its pools of moonlight whirled about her, but he was quite unable to exact a response. Even her eyes refused to meet the blaze of frustrated passion in his and remained tightly shut.

He let her go at last, and her eyes flew open and met his with disdain.

"I think that was contemptible, my lord," she said, "and it's a pity I have to remember you with contempt. If I ever rendered you a service it should have deserved something better than that."

And she sped away from him along the gallery, without his making the smallest effort to detain her.

CHAPTER
TWELVE

THEY left Hollowthorne very early the following morning, before the sun was well up and warming the world, and while there was still an indescribable freshness in the air which Harriet found very pleasing. Lady Fanny was not accustomed to rising at an early hour and her mood was a little peevish, but she was eager to be back in Hill Street with as little delay as possible.

For the house in Hill Street might be small, but it was equipped with everything a widow in her position could possibly need, which caused her friends to envy her. Hollowthorne, in her opinion, was no better than a crumbling ruin set in rural surroundings, and it always depressed her.

Lord Bruce stood in the doorway of the Elizabethan house – very mellow at that hour, Harriet thought, with the rosy red bricks veiled in soft morning mist, and the gardens giving off an entrancing assortment of perfumes—and looked a little wistful as he waved them goodbye. He was leaning on a stick, and his empty sleeve seemed to hang disconsolately at his side. Now that he no longer had a personal manservant and Rawlins had to do duty for a valet as well as acting the part of a general factotum inside the house the folds of his cravat were a little awry, and his general appearance was not as impeccable as it might have been.

Lady Fanny did her best to smile brightly at him, although her conscience was plaguing her a little, but the only comment she made was in connection with the Marquis making no attempt to see them off.

"But then that is all one might expect of Richard," she remarked a little acidly. "After all the inconvenience one has put oneself to over him and his affairs, this is one's reward. Not even a promise to return to London in time to be present at my ball next month."

"Are you giving a ball, my lady?" Harriet asked, feeling some such enquiry was expected of her, although her eyes were on the windows of the house as they turned into the drive – and in particular the great window above the staircase which overlooked the hall, where it was just possible that someone might have been observing their departure.

"Yes, and it is to be a really extravagant affair, given for my niece who will be out this season. One might have thought an uncle would have displayed some small concern for a niece in such circumstances, do you not think?"

Harriet, who could not imagine the Marquis of Capel taking any interest in the affairs of a niece – unless she happened to be remarkably pretty and beguiling – found it necessary to agree. But as she did so she thought she detected a movement at the window at which she gazed so earnestly, and a feeling of extraordinary relief assailed her. The Marquis, after all, was not lying in bed ... Or was he? Was it simply and solely her imagination, coupled with a desire to believe that he might be doing something entirely different, such as observing her departure? Never in all her twenty-two years, until last night, had any man, apart from her father, kissed her cheek ... And the Marquis's hot kisses had seemed literally to scorch her cheek, as well as other areas of her face and throat and hair. Despite her determination to remain apparently as cool as ice, she had known a wild desire to abandon such a pretence and sink into his arms – even to cling to him almost passionately.

Which, no doubt, would have surprised him a good deal, and it was something to be thankful for that she had had the strength to withstand such a temptation, and was being borne away from Hollowthorne without any obvious shattering of her defences.

It was highly unlikely that she would ever see the Marquis again, and for the sake of her peace of mind it was best that she should not do so. But if ever she did meet him again she must – she *must* remain an enigma! It was her one defence against him!

With one last glance upwards at the windows of the house she acknowledged that to herself.

By the time they reached London Lady Fanny was professing herself completely exhausted, and Harriet was feeling so unaccountably depressed that it secretly alarmed her. As the carriage bowled through St. James's Square she tried not to look out for the impressive house on the corner which was the London residence of Lord Capel, but when her eyes alighted on the steps up which she had so recently walked her feeling of depression increased tenfold. She wondered whether she would ever shake it off, and whether it would be possible to continue one's existence in such an atmosphere of profound gloom.

Lady Fanny's housekeeper received them effusively, and Harriet was allotted a very pretty bedroom overlooking the gardens in the square, which diverted her temporarily. She realised she ought to feel extremely grateful because she could call it her own.

The next morning Lady Fanny was up betimes despite her exhaustion of the previous day, declaring that they had much to do. She wished to visit a silk warehouse in the City, and Harriet was to accompany her.

"You must forgive me, my dear, but I find your clothes so very depressing that I have to do something about them," she confessed. "My brother is most anxious to recompense you in some way for all that you have done for him and the – er – de Courceys," she added hurriedly. "But for you and the admirable determination you displayed they would all three be suffering acute privations and Lowthan Hall would be like a beleaguered fort. So you must not put forth any arguments, my dear, if he has left it to me to provide you with a suitable wardrobe. To that end we are setting forth this morning."

Harriet was horrified.

"But, my lady," she protested, "I cannot permit the Marquis of Capel to make himself responsible for the deficiencies in my wardrobe. They are nothing whatsoever to do with him."

Lady Fanny smiled.

"That is perfectly true," she agreed. "But there is such a thing as generosity – and he feels very generously towards you. After all, it is very likely that you saved his life by your skilful nursing, and if you are to look after his ward you must be suitably attired."

"As becomes a governess, surely? And any arrears of salary that are due to me will pay for that."

"Of course, my dear – very sensibly put. Your arrears of salary! They must be quite considerable. After we have visited the silk warehouse we will look in upon a dressmaker who can perform miracles with the most ordinary materials, and after that there will be bonnets and shoes and gloves and so forth. The list is quite endless, and if there is not enough money to pay for it all you shall look upon me as your creditor, and you need have not the least fear in the world that I shall set the duns on to you if repayment is not made within a set period of time."

"So long as there is no question of your brother being responsible for our purchases," Harriet said anxiously, recognising at the same time that Lady Fanny was going to become very difficult to cope with if she insisted on raising objections to this shopping expedition.

Lady Fanny waved a hand airily.

"La, my dear child, you must think me excessively unconventional if you imagine I would approve of Capel purchasing your wardrobe for you. Why, that would place you in the same category as one of his mistresses, and you are far from being that kind of young woman as we are all very well aware." This last remark was made with a certain degree of archness in her look which far from allayed Harriet's fears. "What would Devil Yorke say if his daughter, who had already endangered her reputation by consorting somewhat unwisely with my brother, allowed him to become her creditor?"

"Please, ma'am," Harriet implored, her eyes widening at the very suggestion, "I beg you will not even mention such an unlikely situation!"

"Then I will not do so, my dear." She reached across the breakfast table and patted Harriet's hands. "Now run along and collect your bonnet and let us waste no further time."

The shopping expedition left Harriet feeling even more exhausted than Lady Fanny had professed herself to be on the previous evening. The silk warehouse was so fascinating that Harriet could have devoted hours to examining the tempting fabrics that were brought forth in bales for their consideration. Although Lady Fanny had talked of "perfectly ordinary materials" there were none, so far as Harriet could discover, in this particular emporium that could have answered to such a description. There were delicious satins and lustrings and tiffanys and gauzes that enchanted the eyes, but nothing suitable to make up into a severe little robe for a governess in receipt of a salary. But Lady Fanny pounced on a roll of soft grey silk and announced that it would be simply ideal for a couple of day dresses, and a delicate length of white

muslin appealed to her immediately as the essential basis
for a quite enchanting evening-gown. Harriet was fingering
some pretty cambric which she had more or less decided
privately she could quite well make up herself into an un-
ambitious dress for the approaching summer days, but the
Duke's daughter swept it aside and declared in favour of a
piece of leaf-green crêpe and another length of muslin which
in this instance was worked with delicate thread and was
known, as Lady Fanny explained to her, as jaconet muslin,
and was quite the thing for a young woman of her years.

After the silk warehouse they went on to an establishment
which quite took Harriet's breath away. It was most handsomely carpeted and hung with satin drapes – altogether very
elaborate – and it was here that Lady Fanny insisted on the
purchase of a couple of ready-made dresses which were far
more extravagant than anything Harriet had ever dreamed she
might one day possess. One was of water-green silk em-
broidered with little knots of velvet ribbon, and the other
was of plain light blue satin which lent a curious depth to
Harriet's eyes and drew attention to the delicate texture of her
skin and the soft flush which so often overspread it.

Lady Fanny explained for Harriet's benefit that they were
part of a wardrobe originally intended for the daughter of a
favoured customer who had been obliged to leave London
before the purchases were ready, and had later changed her
mind about them. And by some fortunate chance they were
exactly Harriet's size.

Then the saleswoman brought forth a selection of pelisses
which had also been designed for the same young lady, and
Lady Fanny selected one of grey Berlin silk and another in
dark blue velvet. At another emporium they purchased
half-boots, kid slippers, some very fine silk stockings, and two
enchanting bonnets; and at yet another they acquired gloves
and shawls. Harriet simply could not believe that all these

items were to be worn by herself, and in any case she considered the number of purchases vastly in excess of her needs. When Lady Fanny instructed that the goods were all to be charged to her various accounts she found the courage to protest with some vehemence, but Lady Fanny pinched her cheek and ordered her to forget all about the matter and to take pride instead in her new possessions.

"Believe me, my dear, you are going to create quite a sensation when you make your appearance in all this splendid new finery," she assured her. And when my brother Bruce claps eyes on you in that beguiling bonnet with the rose velvet lining you will have him falling at your feet."

Harriet looked even more anxious.

"But I would not wish Lord Bruce to fall at my feet," she protested. "I consider that he has suffered enough in the service of his country and I would not wish him to – to conceive any ideas about me."

Lady Fanny smiled at her.

"Do you not think it possible that he has already conceived ideas about you?"

"I – I hope not."

"Meaning that that empty sleeve of his offends you?"

"No, no, of course not! But I am Verbena's governess, and as such he will surely see me . . .?"

"Why, yes, of course, my dear," Lady Fanny soothed her, and gave instructions to her coachman to carry them back to Hill Street.

The next morning the dressmaker arrived, and Harriet spent hours standing in front of her in the schoolroom which had been set aside for the use of herself and Verbena, submitting to pins being stuck into her and having her waist pinched in and her shoulders held back by force whenever she displayed a tendency to droop. The dressmaker, a pleasant little woman who plainly delighted in her craft, was very enthusiastic and promised all the dresses within such a short time that Harriet wondered whether she was going to sit up all night and work on them; but Lady Fanny seemed to think it perfectly normal and rational and understandable that the dressmaker should be prepared to damage her eyesight in the interests of anyone connected with such an eminent personage as the Duke of Coltsfoot's only daughter. And as Harriet was a guest in her house an aura of importance began to surround her, too, which did not make her feel entirely happy.

She did feel better a few days later when Verbena arrived from the country. Verbena, from whom she had been parted, for what now seemed to be an excessively long time, was so delighted by the reunion that she hugged her continuously for several minutes, and declared that she had been terrified lest she was never going to see Harriet again. The child was very pretty and had engaging ways, and even Lady Fanny seemed to take to her. Once more she lamented that if the girl had only been a little older she could have done so much for her, but since she was obliged to take an interest in her and had undertaken on her brother's behalf to supervise her upbringing it was very much in Verbena's favour that she was presentable and that she, Fanny, need not feel in the least ashamed of her.

Once some expenditure had been devoted to seeing her suitably attired, she would be prepared to take her up in her own carriage when driving in the park, and if the two boys were as happily manageable then they were welcome to stay with her whenever they were not engaged with their studies.

But for the first few days after Verbena's arrival in Hill Street studies were set aside and Lady Fanny encouraged Harriet to take the child about and let her see a little of the great city, about which she must often have felt curious when living in such a rural county as Sussex. A carriage was placed at their disposal, and the coachman had instructions to take them for drives in the park, and to such edifices as the Tower of London, St. Paul's Cathedral and Westminster Abbey. Verbena was a little afraid of the dimness of the cathedral, but she was rather more intrigued by the Tower of London, and particularly the boats on the river which it overlooked. She loved the high-stepping horses which carried them in style through the park, and hoped that one day her brother Robert might purchase just such a team, and perhaps also a pony for herself – this after she had admired the ladies riding side-saddle in the park, and been considerably intrigued, despite her youth, by the gentlemen who escorted them.

Beside her on the seat of the carriage was an enormous doll, dressed in the very height of fashion, which was her very dearest possession, and which Harriet had been astonished to learn had been presented to her by the Marquis of Capel when he had apparently taken it into his head to visit Lowthan Hall and his three wards after Harriet had departed from Hollowthorne. He must have gone there immediately, Harriet realised. Apparently the Duke had not accompanied him, so he must have ridden over alone from Coltsfoot.

Verbena had been so much impressed by him that she did not need to be pressed for her opinion concerning him when Harriet enquired. She declared rapturously that she had thought he was "very much kinder than Papa", and that in addition to the doll, he had presented her with boxes of sugared confections and some satin ribbons for her hair, and he had promised her a brand-new dress for her birthday, and a pair of high kid boots like those which the daughter of their nearest neighbour already possessed. He had promised Ferdie a new fishing line and his own hunter before the summer was over, and Robert was to acquire a handsome new gun and his own sitting-room at Oxford.

According to Verbena the boys had been as much taken

with their guardian, about whom they had always been intensely curious, as she was herself, and they no longer felt in the least apprehensive about his handling of their affairs, at any rate until Robert came of age. Robert was frankly not looking forward to responsibility so he was perfectly happy about an arrangement whereby the Marquis made his decisions about his young sister's upbringing and his young brother's future education. Apparently both boys had voted him a regular "out-and-outer", in addition to being much impressed by his elegance and dandyism which they considered entitled him to be known as "a Corinthian of Corinthians". Robert was already striving to emulate the manner in which he tied his cravat, without much success, and Ferdie had decided to make a supreme effort to resemble him as closely as possible when he reached his advanced years.

And as for Verbena, she thought him "so much handsomer than Papa," and quite as generous. And as the late Sir Willoughby had indulged his only daughter to such an extent that those near to them had considered he would ruin her character altogether if he continued with so much indulgence, this was quite an admission.

Hugging her doll in her arms and gazing out of the carriage windows with entranced eyes, Verbena added yet another titbit of information to Harriet, confessing happily that the Marquis had promised to invite her to stay with him before very long.

"When he is married," she added. "He is to marry a very beautiful lady before very long, and I am to spend at least a part of every year with them when they are staying in the country. And I shall have a lot of new dresses which I am to choose myself, and a large nursery where there will be other children I can play with, and our governess will be someone very kind whom I shall like very much indeed – almost as much as I like you," giving Harriet's hand a squeeze. "Do you think that Lord Capel is thinking of you, Miss Yorke? When I asked him he smiled and said I would have to wait and find out."

"Did – did he say that?" Harriet enquired, rather faintly.

"Oh, yes. And when I told him I would rather have you than anyone else he said it was just possible that you, too, would be getting married. But you're not, are you? You're not going to get married and go away and leave me again?"

"I have no intention of doing anything of the kind at the moment, or indeed in the foreseeable future," Harriet reassured her.

"And does 'foreseeable future' mean that you won't ever get married?"

"I think it is very likely that that is what it could mean."

"Then Cook must be right," Verbena exclaimed with satisfaction, "for when you went off to London and didn't come back she said that of course you would come back sooner or later for governesses had to earn their living, and what else would you do if you didn't return to Lowthan Hall? She didn't seem to think you would get married."

"She must have been looking at the tea-leaves again," Harriet replied, absentmindedly watching one small dog chasing another across the open spaces of the park.

Lord Bruce arrived in London a few days later, and presented himself in Hill Street. He had smartened himself up so very considerably that Harriet was quite amazed. In place of his country attire he wore a new bright blue coat and well-fitting pantaloons, and he looked as if he had just left the hands of a really experienced valet, which must mean, she thought, that he had established himself in some temporary headquarters in the capital and was proposing to lead a very different kind of life from that which he had led in the country.

In confirmation of her assumption, Lord Bruce admitted that he had no plans to return to Hollowthorne immediately.

Since he was of no further use in the Army he had decided to try a different style of living, and his sister had suggested he should shun solitude for a while and take an interest in Society. He had never previously been interested in Society but – damn it all! – he wasn't a helpless cripple just because he had lost an arm, and who knew what the future might have in store for him if he ceased bemoaning his lot? He recognised that he wasn't the only one who had suffered at Waterloo, and that there were a number of people in the world who wouldn't despise him.

He looked with such open admiration at Harriet that, although she stammered in agreement, she felt acutely uncomfortable as a result of his arrival. She was wearing one of her new grey silk dresses, and with her chestnut curls caught modishly up on to the top of her head and secured there with a velvet ribbon – an attempt on the part of Lady Fanny's maid to turn her into a fashionable young woman – she presented an appearance of charming sophistication which might well have overcome an Army officer who had once been accustomed to meeting many pretty ladies but had been denied that pleasure for so long. His capacity for recognising exceptional merit was as sharp as ever and Lord Bruce had been hit in a very vulnerable spot the moment he met the limpid greenness of Harriet's clear gaze.

He accepted an invitation from his sister to stay to dinner, and afterwards he arranged to collect Harriet and Verbena the following day and take them on another expedition to discover more of the sights of London.

Verbena thoroughly enjoyed the outing, but Harriet was left feeling a trifle fatigued. She had already seen Madame Tussaud's wax museum on two previous occasions, and she was not as enthusiastic about the Royal Mint as she might have been, although it certainly proved instructive to her charge. They went on to stand beneath the whispering gallery in St. Paul's, and explored a narrow network of streets in the heart of the City, which left them feeling distinctly footsore. The following day, since Lady Fanny insisted on it, Lord Bruce again escorted them, and this time it was Lord Elgin's collection of marbles at Burlington House which was the highlight of their morning's entertainment. This proved highly diverting to Harriet, although she privately considered it was not an ideally suitable exhibition for a child fresh from the country, particularly in the company of a comparatively unknown gentleman. In the afternoon they went on to the British Museum which once again was instructive, and after that, because Verbena particularly desired it, they returned to the Tower of London, where Lord Bruce took pains to explain to the child as many details as he could recollect about the princes who had been incarcerated there, and the ravens that haunted Tower Green.

Verbena's eyes grew wide and fascinated as she listened, and Harriet was a little afraid she might have nightmares that night, but nothing of the kind occurred.

After that expedition even Lord Bruce was limping more noticeably than he usually did, and this provided Harriet with a perfectly sound excuse for refusing his escort the next day. In addition to that the dressmaker was once more visiting them, this time to create a wardrobe for Verbena, who was highly excited by the prospect of possessing many new dresses in pretty muslins and ginghams. So Lord Bruce went off, not entirely depressed, to begin a round of his clubs and hitherto neglected acquaintance. But before he did so he exacted a promise from Lady Fanny that she would allow him to make up a party for the theatre, which would of course include Harriet, and which would be followed by supper at one of the more discreet restaurants, the popularity of which he could vouch for.

Harriet wore her pale blue satin for the theatre outing, and as it was her first experience of sitting in a box and being viewed with open interest by the people sitting opposite she found it a little disconcerting, particularly as the other members of her own party did much the same thing from time to time. Lady Fanny had insisted on lending Harriet a pearl necklace, and provided her with a little pearl-handled fan with which to deflect the glances of the curious when they became overwhelming. Lord Bruce, sitting beside her, stared fixedly at her throughout the performance. In his opinion, the shimmer on her chestnut hair from the subdued lighting and the lustre of the pearls nestling against her creamy throat were far more fascinating and deserving of his attention than the actors who preened and postured before them.

Harriet thoroughly enjoyed the play, but she would have enjoyed it still more if Lord Bruce had not been so attentive. At supper afterwards he was even more so since champagne was served and Harriet, quite unaccustomed to it, merely sipped at hers, while everyone else drank liberally. Lady Fanny beamed, as if everything about the evening was entirely satisfactory to her, and whenever her eyes encountered Harriet's the latter became convinced they were sparkling with both secret amusement and genuine pleasure. When Lord Bruce left them in Hill Street he said that he would call upon them the following morning, and his sister replied immediately that naturally he would remain and take a light luncheon with them. He could escort Miss Yorke to the park, and there was a little shop in Bond Street where she could match her new kid slippers with gloves of exactly the same hue.

"I am sure she will be delighted if you will accompany her there," she said.

But Harriet protested immediately:

"But, ma'am, have you forgotten that Verbena is being fitted for her new pelisse? And Miss Frobisher has not enough silk for the redingote she is to make for her – I was proposing to visit the silk warehouse and see if a match can be obtained."

Lady Fanny shrugged dismissingly.

"Nonsense, my dear, Miss Frobisher can attend to all that. It will be much pleasanter in the park."

Harriet turned away, alarmed for the first time because it seemed to her – indeed, it was becoming increasingly clear – that her life was being taken over and that she was being allowed less and less freedom to make her own decisions. Since leaving Lowthan Hall so much had happened to her that she was more than a little bewildered, and when she met Lord Bruce's eyes – honest and brown and appealing – she began to feel genuinely frightened. His admiration for her was so very transparent, that Lady Fanny approved of his admiring her, so that unless she was very strong-minded she might find herself whirled into a situation from which there would be no possibility of escape.

She thought of the Marquis of Capel and although he was probably miles away her lips started to burn at the memory of his kisses. But astonishingly enough that recollection was a salutary thing, and she heard herself stammering awkwardly,

"Of course, ma'am, if – if Lord Bruce is prepared to devote to me so much of his time."

Lord Bruce bowed, and regarded her with faint reproach.

"As if, Miss Yorke, I could do anything else," he said with reproach in his voice as well.

For the next two weeks he was a constant caller in Hill Street, and although Harriet now received remuneration for looking after Verbena and supervising her daily lessons and walks and other diversions, she was constantly deprived of the opportunity to carry out these duties faithfully in a manner which satisfied her conscience. There was always a housemaid to take over most functions (apart, that is, from the lessons), and even the cook obliged by entertaining Miss Verbena in the kitchen. This meant that the child was regaled with in-digestible cakes and tarts and home-made orange cordial while Cook indulged her weakness for highly-priced tea and determined the pattern her future was to take by studying the tea-leaves left at the bottom of her cup. On more than one occasion she offered to perform this service for Harriet, who refused, while rebelling inwardly because the orderly walk to watch the riders in the Row, or the ladies in their carriages, was denied her. Lord Bruce almost inevitably arrived whenever she was planning to set forth after a reviving shower of rain or in the pleasant warmth of an early summer evening, either to act as her escort or to detain her in the library for a talk, which he endeavoured to make as intimate as possible, con-cerning the manner in which she was passing her time.

And even if she succeeded in avoiding him in Hill Street she was bound to encounter him in Piccadilly, or in the Green Park, or in a favourite bookshop, or even on one occasion while choosing ribbons for Lady Fanny in a fascinating em-porium in Bond Street which she had visited previously in her charge.

As he was always so embarrassingly pleased to see her, and so excessively gratified if she accorded him even a half smile, that she began to feel as if some skilfully contrived web was closing round her.

She was prepared to admit that she admired Lord Bruce tremendously, that his war record was something her father would have loved to hear about, that she sympathised with his injured foot and his lack of one arm, and that she even enjoyed talking to him – occasionally. But Lady Fanny's insistence that she should entertain him on every possible occasion was beginning to affect her like a nightmare.

She was not afraid of remaining a spinster, and she did not intend to marry Lord Bruce. And Lord Bruce, she was certain, was daily coming nearer to making her an offer of marriage.

The Season was getting into its stride, and all sorts of parties and balls and routs were taking place daily. London was a hive of activity, and the atmosphere of liveliness and gaiety was infectious. Lady Fanny's proposed ball for her niece was to take place on the last day of May, and since the house in Hill Street was so small Lord Capel was lending his house in St. James's Square for the occasion. Lady Fanny became immersed in preparations for this event, and Harriet was required to lend her as much assistance as possible. There were guest lists to be drawn up, invitations to be written and despatched, flowers to be ordered and confectioners to be consulted, to say nothing of the vital business of ordering all the food and the wines. It was such an important and highly esteemed affair that no detail could be overlooked, and visits to St. James's Square were undeniably necessary.

On the occasion of the first visit Lady Fanny invited Harriet to accompany her. Pauncefoot opened the door to them, but apart from a faint glimmer of surprise in his eyes Harriet could not be entirely certain that he recognised her. The house was dust-sheeted and silent, a faint odour of disuse following them as they paraded through the rooms.

Harriet recognised the little anteroom where she had been incarcerated for over an hour, and she of course recognised the library immediately. It seemed even more oppressive than the other rooms, opulent beyond belief with its gilded cornices and its ornate arches, the flowing velvet curtains before the windows and the deep leather chairs. The great desk was carefully shrouded in a holland cover, but it took little effort on her part to see the Marquis seated behind it, reaching for his writing materials, regarding her with those velvety dark eyes of his. His dark blue coat and his impeccably fitting white satin waistcoat were there before her eyes, just as she so plainly saw his shapely hands with the carefully tended nails mending an awkward pen which he was preparing to take upstairs with him to his room, and then casting it aside impatiently. She watched him pick up another ...

Lady Fanny turned to her. Harriet did not realise that she studied her for a long time, with considerable interest, before she spoke. And when she spoke Harriet started so violently that she found it necessary to apologise.

"I was thinking what a – what a very handsome desk that is!" she said.

Lady Fanny smiled strangely.

"It is over-large for the room, but I'm afraid my brother has somewhat unconventional tastes. I personally could not endure to have a room so ponderously ornate as this in my house. I would call upon someone with the most modern ideas and a great deal of skill to refurnish it for me, and of course I could not endure for a moment those dreadful leather chairs," waving a hand to indicate them. "They are most cumbersome and in every way offensive to the eye –"

"But very comfortable," Harriet heard herself say defensively, recalling that she had occupied one of them for far longer than she had believed she would be able to endure, and that she had been petrified lest the owner of the house had her ejected by force.

Lady Fanny smiled again and pinched her cheek.

"Oh, yes, of course, I forgot that you have seen this room before. And no doubt it had a different aspect while you were concealed behind the curtains."

"Will – will the Marquis of Capel be attending your niece's ball?" Harriet enquired, not in the least certain why she had to ask such a question.

"I should think not. No, I am fairly certain he will not, since for one thing Annabel is not his niece – she is the daughter of my late husband's widowed sister – and for another he is so much preoccupied at Capel that I'm sure he will have little time to spare. I am given to understand that they have quite a party there, and Rowena Harmsworth is at her most radiant and beguiling everyone who has not already succumbed to her charms. So you may be sure Capel would be very loath to leave such excellent entertainment. And certainly he would not regard a young girl's coming-out as of very much importance."

"I see," Harriet said.

Lady Fanny subjected her to a quizzing look, and then walked briskly to the open door.

"Well, come along, my dear, we have much to do," she said. "We have not yet inspected the ballroom, and there is the question of deciding upon a room for the card players ... If my memory serves me we always used the Purple Drawing-room. It is not too large, and if the night is cold we can always see to it that there is a good fire."

CHAPTER
THIRTEEN

ON the night in question there was no need of a fire, for the last days of May were unseasonably warm. Lady Fanny complained that it was quite oppressive, and she would not have been in the least surprised if, at the height of the ball, the heavens opened and the garden which provided some delightfully tucked-away nooks and corners for lovers was drenched by a sudden downpour. At the same time she was grateful for the garden from which she was able to gather numbers of fresh blooms to supplement the quantities arriving in baskets from local florists, which filled the great house with a steadily increasing fragrance.

The task of arranging these flowers was allotted to Harriet, and it was she who decorated the long tables in the supper-room with white and yellow roses. The Grecian figures in the hall were also garlanded with roses, and great sheaves of purple iris strained towards the painted ceiling. Lady Fanny was most impressed. She was even more impressed when Harriet decided the staircase should be banked with white camellias, and the little gallery where the orchestra would set up their instruments was transformed into a kind of flowery bower also.

"My dear," she declared, "you have quite a knack with these things. You will make quite a remarkable hostess one of these days."

Harriet, while she appreciated the compliment, saw no necessity to comment on such an unlikely event, and Lady

Fanny suggested she should return to Hill Street and order a late luncheon for herself and her hostess, when it would be time to begin the business of her toilet which, from her ladyship's own experience, was likely to take a considerable while. Harriet was glad to escape to her room, where the dress she was to wear that evening was already spread out on the bed, and Lady Fanny's maid was attaching some white satin ribbons and a cluster of silver rosebuds to the high waistline.

The dress was a present from Lady Fanny, one the Duke's daughter had insisted on making to Verbena's governess, and Harriet could hardly believe that she would be wearing it. It was of white silk gauze, as transparent as the wings of a moth, although underneath it was a long satin petticoat which prevented her feeling uncomfortably naked – although Lady Fanny herself frequently shocked her friends by her daring mode of dress. Verbena, released from her lessons that day, was enchanted by the dress, and she begged permission to remain with Harriet until her toilette was completed and Lady Fanny's carriage was at the door to convey them to St. James's Square.

For the first time Harriet saw the Marquis of Capel's great town house at its best – as it must often have appeared in the past. It was not yet quite dusk, but lights streamed from the house and a strip of bright scarlet carpet extended from the front door to the pavement where the guests would alight from their carriages and sedans. An awning of similar colour, much embossed with gold thread, was stretched above it. In the brilliantly lighted entrance hall Pauncefoot, resplendent in the Marquis's livery of green and gold, stood prominently at the head of his little band of similarly attired footmen, and the moment Lady Fanny was assisted from her carriage he darted forward to receive her with exaggerated bows and gyrations, his magnificently powdered head bent almost to the dust at her feet. As Harriet followed her up the steps he unbent sufficiently to cast her an appraising glance. His eyes grew wider as he took in the details of her gauze and satin, with Lady Fanny's pearls crowning the whole effect, and Harriet smiled at him in a completely understanding manner, recollecting how mistrustful of her he had been when she had dared to request an interview with the Marquis one recent Sunday morning.

If Pauncefoot also recollected that morning – which he undoubtedly did – nothing was given away by his expression. His attitude to her, as well as Lady Fanny, could not have been more subservient. Harriet recognised that this was a real triumph.

The evening commenced with the arrival of the first guests. Lady Fanny had already taken up her position at the head of the grand staircase, with her niece Annabel standing shyly on her right hand to be presented to each guest in turn. Lady Fanny's appearance was sufficiently startling to merit more astonished glances in her direction than were ever directed at the fair-haired young girl in her drifts of white muslin and pale blue silk roses who was supposed to be the centre of attention for the evening; but since she was almost painfully shy, this no doubt was something for which Annabel herself was grateful. Only when the orchestra started up, and the first young man – carefully vetted beforehand by Lady Fanny herself – asked her to dance, did Annabel's expression lighten, and within a short time she was enjoying herself hugely and the ball was pronounced a success.

Harriet, with no official status and therefore introduced very casually to a comparatively limited number of people, was able to appreciate the novelty of the experience right from the outset, and when Lord Bruce appeared at her elbow in all the glory of his regimentals and announced that he proposed to devote himself to her for the entire evening she was able to relax completely and enjoy herself. The music was lively, but owing to his disability the Duke of Coltsfoot's younger son was unable to dance, so Harriet accompanied him quite happily into the conservatory where they sat amongst the trailing vines and the potted plants and listened to the music and talked.

The talk was desultory, for Harriet's foot was tapping unconsciously in time to the quadrille and the country dances, to say nothing of the latest innovation, the highly controversial waltz. To follow intelligently such subjects as farming in Wiltshire and fishing in Sussex rivers became a little difficult after a time. Lord Bruce decided she was in need of some refreshment and left her to procure a glass of negus or lemon-water, which she said she would prefer as it was warm inside the conservatory. It was during his absence that a gentleman who had been observing her with a certain amount of pleasure while she was seated with the mamas in the ballroom came in hopefully to enquire whether she would be so good as to stand up with him in the polka, which according to the programme was to be the next item.

Harriet, who would have loved nothing better than to dance the polka with almost any unknown gentleman at that moment, shook her head and smiled regretfully. She thanked him and declared that she was not dancing.

The gentleman withdrew. A few seconds later, another slightly younger man made his appearance and actually ventured to argue with her when once again she shook her head and informed him that she had no intention whatsoever of taking the floor. His downcast looks very nearly caused her to change her mind, but the recollection that Lord Bruce would be returning at almost any moment enabled her to be quite firm. The young gentleman departed, wondering why it was that the prettiest ones were always the most difficult to persuade, having decided that Harriet was "damned nearly the prettiest one at the ball".

Unfortunately for Harriet, who was growing a little tired of her incarceration in the conservatory, Lord Bruce had run into a brother officer in the refreshment room. As he was also a veteran of Waterloo and the two had not seen one another for some time, they had quite a lot to talk about and Lord Bruce found it difficult to get away. He had every intention of going in search of lemon-water as soon as the moment presented itself, but for the time being his friend had attached himself very firmly, and although Harriet was far from forgotten he hoped she would wait patiently for his return.

But Harriet was haunted all at once by her memories of that night in the library and all that had followed as a result of it. The music was making her feel acutely restless and, combined with the knowledge that this was the Marquis of Capel's house, that the very chair she sat on belonged to him and the smooth lawn outside the windows was one which he had frequently trodden, somehow affected her in an intolerable way. Finally, she suddenly jumped up from her chair and started pacing restlessly up and down, prey to uncomfortably clear visions of the Marquis's handsome face.

She felt suddenly stifled by the atmosphere inside the conservatory, and wrenched open the door which led to the garden. Lady Fanny had talked of secret nooks and arbours which might appeal to lovers, but as she stole along the paths beneath the stars it seemed to her that she had the garden to herself. There was no one about, and behind her in the house the dancing seemed to be at its height, the music so entrancing that apparently no one was willing to forgo a single moment of it. Harriet, a slender wraith in her white dress, with the silver roses nestling at her waist and a real white rose caught up in her curls, stood very still in the middle of a path which apparently led to nowhere, apart from a little arbour shrouded in palest jasmine flowers. The waning crescent of a young moon hung in the sky above, and Harriet paused to admire it, and to think how sweet and fresh the night air was – how wonderfully reviving after the close confinement of the conservatory.

Something moved near the arbour, and she realised that it was one of Lady Fanny's romantically-minded couples who had emerged on to the steps which led down to the paved walk. The man was exceptionally tall with well-held shoulders, and even in the indifferent light the arrogance of his head and the curious clarity of his dark profile struck her as remarkably similar to an attitude and features she had come to know very well in recent weeks. His companion was an exquisitely slender and graceful creature in a shimmering gown, and her arm was linked in that of her escort. Before they descended the steps she paused and stood on tiptoe to look directly up into his face, the disparity in their height being quite considerable, and to Harriet's horror – because she was quite unable to avoid acting the part of an audience – after a light and provocative laugh which rang like silver bells in the silence of the night, she kissed him deliberately.

The Marquis of Capel's response – and Harriet had no doubt at all that it was the Marquis – was immediate. He promptly clasped her in his arms, and in return for that one seductive kiss he kissed her so many times that Harriet, petrified in the middle of the path, could not doubt his ardour. With the memory of similar kisses pressed on her own face at no distant date rushing up to cover her in a wave of excruciating embarrassment, she turned and ran back along the path like a frenzied nymph until she reached the door to the conservatory.

It was most mercifully empty of anyone who looked in the least like Lord Bruce with a glass of lemon-water in his hand, or any other gentleman likely to implore her to dance with him, so she took refuge in a bowery corner of it where there was an enormous palm tree. She pressed herself behind the stout trunk until the lovers from the arbour had entered shortly after her and made their way into the ballroom.

Even after that she refused to desert the protection of her palm tree, and it was many minutes before a measure of her normal composure had been restored to her. One thing was certain: she could no longer face the light-hearted company in the ballroom, and even the prospect of seeing Lord Bruce now struck her as more than she could endure. It did occur to her to wonder what had happened to him after he had gone in search of refreshment for her, but his reason for absenting himself was of no importance. She felt as if some dreadful final humiliation had deprived her of all of her dignity, and more than anything she wanted to escape from the house. So badly did she wish to leave that she was looking round from behind the palm tree like a wild creature in an attempt to decide the best means by which she could achieve this desire without attracting any attention to herself, when a voice called her name, somewhat peremptorily. She knew at once that it was not Lord Bruce trying to discover where she was hiding.

"Miss Yorke!" the masculine voice called. "I believe you expressed a wish for a glass of lemon-water."

Harriet remained hidden, very still and silent.

The Marquis of Capel sighed.

"How contrary women are," he complained. "My brother has been waylaid by a bevy of stout matrons, and I'm afraid it is unlikely he will free himself from their clutches for some considerable while – perhaps not until the supper-dance, which I believe you have promised him. But in the meantime I have given him my word that I will see to it that your desire for this wholesome stimulant is not overlooked, and I beg you to come forth from that tangle of vines and receive it from my hands. I'm afraid I have spilled a little of it . . ." dusting a few trickles from his immaculate person with an even more immaculate handkerchief "but I'm sure you will forgive me. If you are really thirsty . . ."

Harriet stepped forth tentatively, with a frozen face, from her place of concealment. She had decided that there was no dignity in cowering away from him.

"Thank you, my lord," she said, and held out her hand for the lemon-water.

The Marquis relinquished it. He continued to dab lightly at his white satin waistcoat with his handkerchief.

"A curious concoction," he remarked, "lemon-water." His eyes were on her gauzy gown, and in particular he noted the white rose in her hair, and the silver roses at her waist. "Very nice," he commented. "Very, very nice!"

"Thank you, my lord," she replied stiffly.

"But it is no thanks to me," he assured her. "Apparently my sister has been taking a feverish interest in you, and she appears to have presented you with one of her spare pearl necklaces. I hope you will take care of it – it is quite valuable, I assure you."

Harriet felt the colour creeping slowly, painfully over her face and neck.

"It is merely loaned to me, my lord," she assured him. "And you may have every confidence that I shall take the greatest possible care of it," she added, stung by that reference to the value of the necklace she was wearing.

But the Marquis merely smiled.

"I was simply advising you to be a little cautious, because on occasions such as this there are frequently light-fingered gentry let loose among us who might very well deprive you of anything of value if they considered you might make it easy for them. And although you say my sister has loaned it to you I'm sure she will beg your acceptance of it before very long. As Bruce's wife you will need a few trifles like that to keep up your spirits. It is a thousand pities he is a younger son, for you would do great credit to the family jewels. . . ."

"I have no intention of marrying Lord Bruce, even if – even if he desired to marry me," Harriet protested, convinced that he was goading her.

Lord Capel continued to smile, his dark eyes more brilliant and lustrous in the subdued light of the conservatory than she had ever known them before.

"Quite so, quite so," he agreed amiably. "But your intention might yet change, and in case you have not already suspected it my sister Fanny is of a most resolute turn of mind. She has taken a prodigious fancy to you, and is perfectly convinced you will make us both an admirable sister-in-law. She will not allow you to escape her clutches unless you are very, very clever... and think what a devoted husband Bruce will make! The poor fellow may be handicapped by that limp of his, and by his lack of an arm, but he is an exceptionally brave and upright man with a very distinguished record. You could hardly do better than marry him, you know."

Harriet bit her lip.

"I have the greatest possible admiration for Lord Bruce," she confessed. "I think he is the – the nicest man I have ever met."

The Marquis shrugged.

"Well, then? What are you waiting for? His sincere protestations that he will adore you always? I promise you you won't have to wait long for those! And there is always the possibility that if I do not produce an heir, and someone like our friend Aintree picks me off, you will in time become the Duchess of Coltsfoot. Think of that! Little Harriet Yorke, the brave admiral's daughter, a duchess! Surely your father would approve of that?"

"You mock me, my lord," Harriet said stiffly, and with the faintest perceptible quiver in her voice. "For some reason it amuses you to do so."

"Not at all."

The Marquis produced a snuff-box, an elegant affair of gold and ivory, and took a pinch of snuff. He regarded her from beneath those shapely black brows as he did so.

"But there is one thing we must not forget," he remarked, dusting a little of the mixture from the front of his dark blue velvet coat. "I think you have already observed me tonight with the lady who is to become my fiancée, the very beautiful and, despite her diminutive size – not unlike you, when one comes to think of it, Harriet! – surprisingly lusty arouser of the most ardent passions in my breast, Lady Rowena Harmsworth! If she does not produce sons then I will never again lay a wager at White's. In addition to sons she will probably produce quite a few daughters as well, but that is rather like looking into the future, and I prefer not to do that at this present. I prefer to concentrate on yourself, for I feel that I owe you so much, Harriet – and I would not wish you to be under any sort of misapprehension . . ."

"Please, my lord," Harriet begged, attempting to thrust past him, "I would like to return to the ballroom."

But he successfully prevented her doing anything of the kind by placing himself full in her path.

"Naturally," he agreed, "and you shall do so when we have got this problem of your future nicely and tightly tied up. But at the moment it appears to be wandering off at a tangent, and although I am well aware that Fanny expects me to ask that child Annabel to stand up with me in the cotillion which immediately precedes the supper-dance, I cannot do so with an easy mind while you are proving so extraordinarily uncooperative. Perhaps if I talked to you a little about Bruce – what a charming small boy he was, very devoted to his grandmother and always kind to animals . . ."

"*Please*, my lord!" Harriet insisted, wondering whether she could dart past him quickly enough to escape any retaliatory action if that clump of camellias in the painted tub was not so much in her path. Perhaps if she hesitated no longer. . . .

As if he read her thoughts Lord Capel's hand came out and he placed it firmly but lightly on her bare arm, gripping it sufficiently to secure her presence but not exerting the amount of pressure that would bruise her flesh.

"The light is poor in here," he murmured as if the thought occasioned him satisfaction, while he studied her carefully through the gloom. "If we retreated behind that palm tree which protected you before, we would be quite unlikely to be disturbed while we continue this conversation along lines which might lead us to some mutually acceptable arrangement for your future. By which I mean how much longer you must act the part of governess to that little witch Verbena, and whether it is entirely suitable that you should remain in Hill Street . . ."

"Ah, there you are!" Lord Bruce's smooth tones proclaimed with relief as he entered the conservatory hurriedly. "I have been searching for you everywhere, Miss Yorke, and Capel said he would aid me to find you. I see he has been successful. I hope you did not imagine for one single instant that I had forgotten your lemon-water?"

His eyes were on the Marquis's right hand, which had not yet dropped back to his side, although Harriet was standing rigidly in his partial hold, and it was quite plain she was an unwilling prisoner. As for the Marquis, his dark eyes had a smouldering, resentful gleam in them. If he had ever in his life been really delighted to see his brother, this was plainly not such an occasion.

"If your military laurels rested on your capacity for running to earth an evasive but perfectly logical young woman you would be hard put to it to cover yourself with even a small amount of glory," he commented acidly. "My dear Bruce, you must remember that Miss Yorke *is* logical, and when she found it increasingly stuffy here in the conservatory she wandered out into the garden. I saw her with my own eyes. You should have thought of such a contingency, since it was you who actually deserted her."

Lord Bruce looked quite horrified by such a suggestion.

"My dear Miss Yorke," he protested, "I do beg you to believe that it was much against my will that I was detained. An old friend, a campaigner like myself, buttonholed me in the refreshment room, and I'm afraid we had much to talk about. I agree it was highly reprehensible of me to allow myself to be detained, but if you can see your way to forgive me . . .?"

"Of course, Lord Bruce," she said hastily; "it was nothing, I assure you."

"But was it not a little damp in the garden? The dew," he explained.

"It was quite delightful," she assured him. "And I think others – " with a meaningful look at Lord Capel – "enjoyed it, too."

The Marquis released her arm and bowed to her.

"Forgive me if I cannot ask you to stand up with me in the cotillion, Miss Yorke," he begged her stiffly, "but I am already engaged for that long-awaited number. Perhaps if you examine your programme you might find there is a vacant space you can allot to me after the supper-dance. I'm sure Bruce will not wish to be deprived of the delight of taking you in to supper."

When he had left them alone in the conservatory Lord Bruce looked at Harriet a little ruefully.

"I'm afraid I earned that rebuke from my brother," he admitted unhappily, "and I'm sure I do not deserve the honour of taking you in to supper. But perhaps afterwards we can arrange for you to participate a little more fully in the delights of the evening, by which I mean that you must accede to the requests of several young gentlemen who are here this evening and who have been protesting to me that I have been reserving you most unfairly for myself. The fact that I have collected one or two war wounds does not entitle me to monopolise you, and Richard was right to make me feel exceedingly guilty. Now, let us return to the ballroom where we can at least watch the cotillion, and afterwards I shall insist on presenting to you some prospective partners."

He was as good as his word, and the rest of the evening passed for Harriet in a far more lively manner than it had done hitherto. She had been secretly yearning to take a more active part in the dance, instead of sitting in a plush-lined chair on the fringe of the floor watching others enjoy themselves. After watching Lord Capel and Lady Rowena performing gracefully in the cotillion while looking as if it was a natural and normal part of their lives – albeit Rowena, a dazzling fair-haired beauty, looked a trifle bored, as if something about the evening did not entirely please her – she was aware of a strange urgency to be actively engaged rather than sitting and pondering on the recent interview in the conservatory. Poor Lord Bruce was extremely abject every time he recollected how badly she had been deprived. Even if Lord Bruce had become a very open admirer, neither he nor Lady Fanny could protect her from the increasingly violent antagonism she sensed in Lord Capel, or his capacity for reducing her to a state of profound mental confusion.

If he had had a grudge against her, apart from any lingering resentment her involvement in his duel might still cause him, he could not have reacted more unpleasantly than he had done tonight after he had deliberately run her to earth in his own conservatory. According to her lights she had done nothing to deserve it, and she was afraid to think of what might happen if she ever did something positive to arouse his ire.

That he could be violent she more than suspected. That he was not entirely reliable she more than suspected, also.

When the evening was over Annabel was the one who emerged as a completely happy participant in all the pleasures that had been provided. And as the ball had been given in her honour this was not surprising. Lady Fanny, however, ran her close second in proclaiming her entire satisfaction with the evening. As she and Harriet drove back to the diminutive domain in Hill Street in the early hours of the morning, accompanied by Lord Bruce, the Duke's daughter's somewhat startlingly plumaged head, with diamonds and rubies interspersed between the feathers, ceaselessly dipped and waved with every enthusiastic movement she made, while she gestured with her bejewelled hands and arms. If she had had pure French ancestry, she could not have been more addicted to Continental posturings, but Harriet was by this time fully accustomed to her. So she was not entirely deceived by Lady Fanny's excited comments on the ravishing appearance Lady Rowena had presented, the quality of her jewels and the breathtaking beauty of her gown. She was quite convinced that her own jewels were far superior to those of anyone else she knew, and her own gown had created far more interest – even if it was slightly shocking – than any gown worn by any woman present that night in the lavishly decorated rooms of the St. James's Square house.

The fact that she thought it necessary to dilate so extravagantly on Lady Rowena did strike Harriet as having a particular kind of significance. As she was well aware what that significance was, she felt herself growing more and more depressed as the distance lengthened between them and the St. James's Square house (where the Marquis was to remain for that night at least, while Lady Rowena returned to her parents' house in Grosvenor Square), and in the chilling half-light of early dawn she found it difficult to rise above that depression and tell herself that she was being utterly absurd.

It was her first experience of an evening spent exclusively in

the company of the nobility, where a display of wealth and all
its accompanying advantages was prized above everything
else, and now that it was over she had to admit to herself that
she had not been as impressed as she might have been. She felt
as if a bubble had been pricked, and in the grey light Lady
Fanny's plumes – one of which tickled the back of her neck
each time she made a violent gesture – struck her as a little
tawdry, just as the tinsel roses at her own waist struck her as
tawdry. In a corner of the carriage beside her Lord Bruce
nodded and dozed, and finally fell completely asleep, and his
sister reached in front of her and prodded him impatiently
with her fan.

How ridiculous, she declared, for him to behave as if he was
quite unaccustomed to such diversions, when a man of his
years should be living his life to the full. She really would have
to see to it that there was an improvement in his way of life.
He had been shut away at Hollowthorne for too long, far longer than his experiences in the Army had made necessary, and
she really must make it her business to put an end to his year-
nings for solitude. After these remarks, she gazed a little re-
proachfully at Harriet, and then announced that they had
arrived and she simply couldn't wait to be rid of all her tire-
some finery, and if she was not allowed to sleep undisturbed
for hours she would be an utter wreck.

This prediction should have enabled her to feel a certain
sympathy for her brother who, despite his war wounds, had
acted as a tireless escort to Harriet during her recent explora-
tion of London, and who (although he was several years
younger than his sister), had been forced to look on at others
participating more actively in the joys of the evening, so was
probably even more exhausted as a result. Harriet was prepared to concede that he could have been more greatly
afflicted by boredom than anything else.

He apologised profusely for his lapse when he had handed

both ladies out of the carriage, and Harriet received an exceedingly penitent smile from him.

"I really must take myself in hand," he murmured, squeezing her gloved fingers. "I am getting old before my time."

"That is just what I was observing to Miss Yorke before we succeeded in arousing you," Lady Fanny remarked tartly. "It is a process I am determined to alter, since there is no question of your being old. Why, even Richard is a full year older than you are, and no one in their senses would consider that he is anything but at the very peak of manhood."

"Ah, but then I look older than Richard," Lord Bruce replied with dry truthfulness. "And I certainly," he added, "feel older – or I did until a very few weeks ago," looking down with curious earnestness at Harriet.

He lifted the small gloved fingers he still retained within his clasp to his lips and saluted them gallantly.

"Could it be you, Miss Harriet," he enquired softly, "who has provided me with so much incentive to enjoy life that I am actually feeling a little younger?"

Harriet did not reply, and she did not dare encourage him by raising her eyes to his face. That, she felt, would be almost too cruel, considering the decision she had recently reached.

She said goodnight to him hurriedly, followed Lady Fanny into the house, and climbed the stairs to her own room. By the time she reached it and stood looking out of the window at the grey roofs opposite, the sun was rising in a rosy dawn and the last star had vanished.

She felt curiously unwilling to retire to bed. Her depression returned and she sat disconsolately beside the window to dwell upon the emptiness of her own future.

CHAPTER
FOURTEEN

DURING the following week Harriet devoted herself to Verbena, and when Lord Bruce called and expressed a particular desire to see her she sent him away without the consolation of catching so much as a glimpse of her. Lady Fanny's maid looked distinctly curious when requested to convey a polite but regretful message to his lordship, and Lady Fanny expressed herself quite forcibly when it suddenly dawned on her that the demure governess was actually making it plain that the Duke of Coltsfoot's younger son was not good enough for her.

"I don't think you quite realise how devoted Bruce has become to you," she said bluntly. "He has never, so far as I am aware, been in the least interested in any young woman before you – not seriously, that is to say; and even my papa agreed that you would make him an excellent wife. Does not the idea of becoming Lady Bruce Wendover appeal to you at all? Recollect, before you make the disclaimer which I can tell is on your lips, that a young woman in your position, without friends or fortune, is unlikely to receive such an offer again. And if she has the temerity to turn down such an offer then she is brave indeed."

"I think you are forgetting, ma'am, that Lord Bruce has not so far offered for me," Harriet reminded her demurely, looking at the purse she was busily engaged in netting.

"No, but we are both well aware that it is only a matter of time before he does so – time and opportunity, which only you can grant him."

Harriet set the purse aside and looked up at her gravely.

"My lady," she said quietly, "I think I have told you before that I admire Lord Bruce very much indeed, but nothing would induce me to marry him. Nothing!"

"You prefer to remain a spinster?"

"I am not in the least alarmed by the thought of remaining a spinster."

"It is highly unlikely that you will meet many men willing to overlook your entire absence of fortune, and the fact that you have to work for your living as a governess. They may think you pretty and engaging, and be willing to make a little light love to you when the opportunity offers, but you must accept it from me that *they will not marry you.* The best you can hope for is a tradesman's son, or a farmer's son if you are living in the country, and I cannot see you settling down to rear chickens and sell eggs as a means of providing yourself with the occasional pretty fichu and length of gingham to make a dress. So do think seriously about what I am saying before you hurt poor Bruce by sending him about his business."

The colour flamed high in Harriet's cheeks, and she endeavoured to defend herself.

"Naturally it upsets me very much that Lord Bruce might be hurt if he – if he seriously desires to marry me," she declared. "But it would hurt him even more if I married him knowing that I – if I married him without having any love for him at all, and knowing that I could never love him," she corrected herself hurriedly. "That would be terribly unfair to him, and there must be many women in the world – beautiful women of his own kind – who would be happy to marry him."

"Except that so far he doesn't appear to have found one," was the dry retort.

"But he is bound to find one – one day. . . ."

"And you? You will not marry him?"

"No."

Harriet looked down at her hands, which were now painfully linked in her lap, and she was aware that Lady Fanny was studying her as an object of considerable interest. She had come up to the schoolroom knowing that Verbena was temporarily absent to have what she had described at the outset as "a little talk" with Miss Yorke, and somewhat surprisingly, now that the talk was very frank and open she did not appear to be even mildly displeased with Harriet. She studied her from every angle as if she was greatly intrigued by her, and being finally convinced that Bruce was unlikely to be married in the near future she walked to the window and looked out at the garden which it overlooked. Uneasily, Harriet picked up her netting and watched her. Lady Fanny, rather more startling than usual in emerald green sarcenet and black lace, made an apparently casual observation while she flicked with her fan at a fly crawling over a pane of glass.

"You have heard, no doubt, of my brother's engagement?"

"You – you mean the Marquis's engagement to Lady Rowena?"

"Yes. Not that it is official yet, but we are all aware that it is only a matter of time. I had thought at the ball the other night he might make an announcement, but apparently they had not quite come to a decision. However, the disturbing thing in connection with Richard is that he had a nasty fall from his horse after his return to Capel, and although there were no bones broken he displaced his collar-bone and an arm was injured – unfortunately the arm which was penetrated by a bullet so very recently, as you yourself know very well. They have brought him back to St. James's Square where the family physician will attend him, and I trust that he will make a speedy recovery –"

Harriet had risen to her feet, and all at once she was as white as a sheet. Lady Fanny turned to her in concern.

"My dear child," she exclaimed, "what in the world is amiss with you?"

"L-Lord Capel," Harriet stammered. "You said that he had displaced his collar bone – ?"

"Well, and what of it, my dear? That is hardly likely to despatch him, and although I understand that he is covered in bruises, and there is once more some infection in his arm. . . ."

"Not – serious infection?"

"They are finding it a little difficult to control the fever. That is why he is to be seen by Sir Robert Warburton, who is an expert on that sort of thing. Oh, my dear girl, I am not in the least worried . . . Or I was not worried until last night, when he arrived in St. James's Square. Apparently he suffered a good deal on the journey, and they had the greatest difficulty in getting him upstairs to his room. This morning the housekeeper reported that he had occasional lucid intervals, but otherwise he was quite wild in the head and rambling a good deal . . . not even entirely certain where he was. He – he did, in one of his calmer moments, express a desire to see you – "

Harriet grasped at the back of a chair for support.

"You – you mean that he wishes me to go to him, my lady?"

"Well," and Lady Fanny looked down in a certain amount of embarrassment at the carpet, "naturally we cannot presume on you, and your good nature has been taken so much advantage of in the past, but – you did have an extraordinary capacity for dealing with him, and it appears that the housekeeper is no good at all in a sick room, and the housemaids seem to drive him frantic whenever one of them puts her head in at the door of his bedroom. Our old nurse is too old now to be of much assistance, and it is difficult to find someone at such short notice who is suitable and who could control him in his awkward moods and have sufficient strength of mind to see that he takes his medicine instead of flinging it away, and – and you do appear to have many qualifications that it would be difficult to find elsewhere...."

"Then I will go at once," Harriet announced, when Lady Fanny had run out of words for sheer lack of breath. "If you can find someone to take charge of Verbena I will leave immediately."

"Never bother your head about Verbena," Lady Fanny exclaimed with the greatest possible relief. "She is the least of our worries, and Cook will take charge of her in any case. But are you quite sure you do not feel we are taking an unworthy advantage of you?"

"Of course not." Harriet was amazed at such stupidity when the minutes were ticking away and the Marquis might be sinking deeper and deeper into a state of delirium from which it might be well nigh impossible to rouse him, despite the skill of Sir Robert Warburton. Still clinging to the back of the chair, and with a trace of her colour returning, she added: "If you will order a carriage, my lady, I will go to my room and collect a few of my things, then if you are in agreement I will leave immediately. Fortunately I do have a certain amount of knowledge of sick nursing, and you can rest assured that I will do my best."

Her voice, too, trailed away, and Lady Fanny looked at her with a certain amount of sympathy. She had never seen her so pale before.

"La, my dear," she exclaimed, "you are quite a treasure! Even if you will not marry Bruce I have become quite fond of you, and now I am to be excessively grateful to you."

Harriet made an impatient little gesture, and moved towards the door.

"I – I must not waste any time," she said.

"Of course not, my dear! I will ask the coachman to make as much speed as he can with his horses in order to get you to St. James's Square as quickly as possible."

Harriet was grateful that the coachman obeyed his mistress's orders to the word, and they reached St. James's Square so rapidly that she could hardly believe it when they drew up outside the Marquis's town house. She was too disturbed and anxious to think of that other occasion when she had drawn up in a hackney coach outside that very same house, and even when Pauncefoot opened the door she was too preoccupied to recollect that other occasion when he had done so. It did strike her that he looked at her a little peculiarly, but he was extraordinarily deferential, and it was plain that he was expecting her. He led the way at once to the small anteroom where he had left her before, said that he would not keep her waiting above a few minutes, and left her alone to contemplate the silk-lined walls and the Dresden ornaments. In almost exactly five minutes by the ornamental clock on the mantelpiece he was back, bowing from his portly waist as he might have bowed to Lord Capel himself, and asked her to accompany him to the library.

This surprised Harriet, for she had been expecting to be taken upstairs to the Marquis's bedroom. Alarmed lest matters had deteriorated since she set out from Hill Street, she hastened after the dignified butler and enquired of him breathlessly as they reached the library door:

"H-how is Lord Capel, Pauncefoot? Is there any improvement in his condition?"

Pauncefoot swung wide the library door and looked down at her from his infinitely superior height with a faint but noticeable arch to his eyebrows.

"His lordship is expecting you, miss," he replied, and then added: "Miss Yorke to see you, my lord," and stood aside for her to enter the well-remembered room.

There were still some very handsome flower arrangements in the vases which had survived since the ball, and which still appeared to be fresh. The library curtains were drawn a little over the windows so that it was rather dim, but it was quite impossible to mistake the outlines of the great desk behind which Lord Capel had sat while he prepared to write his farewell letters. And once more he was seated behind the desk, and he didn't look in the least ill, and by no stretch of the imagination did it seem as if he was in need of the attentions of a very eminent physician ... let alone the ministrations of Miss Harriet Yorke.

"Ah, thank you, Pauncefoot," he said dismissingly to the butler, and then stood up behind the desk and acknowledged Harriet's presence with a disarming smile. "How good of you to waste so little time in getting here," he told her. "Pray do come in, Miss Yorke, and sit down. I can't tell you how much I appreciate this extreme solicitude."

CHAPTER
FIFTEEN

HARRIET remained standing very close to the library door. She could hear Pauncefoot retreating discreetly along the corridor, and from the hall the mellow tones of a chiming clock reached her. Eleven o'clock. She had indeed made good time on that painful journey from Hill Street.

She swallowed slightly, feeling as if the muscles of her throat were constricting and choking her. The Marquis's face swam before her eyes, which was absurd because he had never appeared so cool and urbane and so inexpressibly well turned-out by the skilful hands of Fetcham as he did this morning. It must have been reaction to the discovery that he was in no danger at all when she had been imagining him half-dead that brought a strange pricking to her eyes and a faint film of moisture threatened to spill over and run down her cheeks. She gulped again, and blinked her eyes angrily and rapidly . . . At least her dignity need not suffer, even if she had been deceived.

"I have no doubt, my lord," she said huskily, "that you find this very amusing."

The Marquis walked swiftly round the desk and stood in front of her.

"I find nothing amusing," he told her with a complete change of expression. "I am only delighted to make the discovery that you are human at last."

"W-what precisely do you mean by that, my – my lord?"

"Oh, Harriet," he said, shaking his head at her, as one tear did actually spill over despite her endeavours and ran down beside her nose. "Oh, Harriet! That you can so deceive yourself is quite astounding, but that you should attempt to deceive me is past belief. We were virtually thrust into one another's company, we have endured so much together, and yet you cannot accept it that it was all for a very particular purpose. You actually hid behind my window curtains here in this very room and looked on at me when I had very little doubt I would lose my life the following day – and would have done but for you. Aintree meant to kill me, you know, and my promise to my father made it impossible for me to kill him. And now all you can do is weep because I am not as ill as you supposed!"

"Oh, n-no, my lord," she stammered, while the tears quite literally flowed. "I am so glad because you are not – not ill at all!"

"Not noticeably ill," he admitted, "but perhaps not as bright as I might have been after riding all night to get here this morning." He passed her his fine cambric handkerchief. "Otherwise I'd know what to do about all that crying of yours, which is quite disfiguring your nose."

"I'm so – s-sorry, my lord."

He moved a little nearer to her.

"What did Fanny tell you?"

"That you'd been thrown from your horse. . . ."

"A likely story! And as a result they had me brought all the way to London?"

"Y-yes."

"Anything else?"

"That your wound had broken out afresh. The wound in your arm!"

"Ah!" he exclaimed.

He held wide his arms to her, and perhaps because she was still half blinded by her tears she blundered into them. His exquisitely-tied cravat was very quickly reduced to a near ruin as she wept uncontrollably for a few minutes. Then, when the extraordinary comfort of his arms began to have effect, and the feel of his mouth moving softly along her arm soothed her still more, she managed to look up at him and to apologise with limpid eyes for behaving so irrationally, in a manner her late father would have deplored.

"I was so very much afraid I might not get here in time," she confessed. "Lady Fanny was so – so very convincing!"

"Only because we neither of us could think of a way to bring you to your senses, you sweet idiot," the Marquis told her. "I used Rowena shamelessly to make you jealous, but even that didn't appear to work very well. She was most obliging and spent half an hour with me in that summerhouse before you made your appearance, but you were as cool and detached as the north wind when I saw you afterwards. Even poor old Bruce didn't seem to think I'd much of a chance after that, and began to be a little more hopeful for his own chances."

"Then – then he – too . . . ?"

"Yes, I'm afraid he, too . . . Which was generous of him, as he's desperately in love with you!"

"I do like him very much indeed," she admitted, burying her nose in his brutally used cravat.

"But you think you can bear to marry me rather than become Lady Bruce Wendover? Of course, if you feel it is your duty to console Bruce, and if on reflection you decide that you could become sufficiently fond of him . . ."

"No, no, no!" she exclaimed, unashamedly putting back her head and looking up at him in a manner that could not have been more revealing. "But I did see you kiss Lady Rowena, and you kissed her so very many times that you must have enjoyed it, and you were not always particularly nice to me, you know. Although you asked me to marry you when your conscience was troubling you, you made it plain when I declined to accept you that you were very much relieved. I had no doubt of that, and it was because of your attitude that I began to dislike you very much – or thought I did! I even began to – to hate you. . . ."

"And now?" he asked, his dark eyes burning into hers.

"I – I – "

"Say it, Harriet," he urged quietly, as he gently untied the ribbons of her bonnet. "Have the courage to say it before I do. You owe me that much, since you have held me so frequently in contempt."

Harriet took a deep breath, and realised that she was committing herself beyond recall.

"I – I'm very much afraid that I love you with all my heart, my lord," she told him simply at last, and his dark face altered so completely that she knew she would never need to retract those words.

He put his fingers under her chin and lifted it up, and they were far from steady as he did so.

"And I, my dearest love," he told her, "have adored you from the moment I first saw you here in this room! I knew there would never be any other woman in my life but you, however many indiscretions I may have committed in the past. So you must take me for what I am, Harriet, self-centred, arrogant, perhaps, impatient and unworthy – but deeply, almost unbearably in love with you! Now, will you kiss me, my dearest heart?"

Harriet's bonnet slipped, unheeded, to the floor.

Ten minutes or so later there came a discreet tap at the door, and when it was opened Lady Fanny stood looking in on them, beaming in anticipation of what she expected to find, but not entirely certain in her own mind that this was the right moment to put her hopes to the test. She had already dismissed Pauncefoot and told him that she was quite capable of announcing herself, but now that the moment had arrived she looked as if she might very readily take flight if circumstances proved to be adverse and she herself unwelcome.

"My dears," she declared as the Marquis partially released Harriet, "I shall take no offence whatsoever if you would prefer that I withdraw and occupy myself in some useful manner until you are ready to discuss pressing matters with me. But if we are to leave for Capel while there is still plenty of daylight I think we should not delay unduly."

And then as the Marquis smiled at her she went forward and prepared to embrace Harriet.

"So I was right after all," she said softly, as a violently blushing Harriet endeavoured to restore some order to her curls. "You are far from being as indifferent to him as you would have us all believe!"

"She is not in the least indifferent to me, I give you my word," the Marquis said triumphantly as he saluted his sister's hand in gratitude. "It was not even necessary for me to take to my bed to have her displaying every sign of contemplating her own early demise if nothing could be done to save me. And now let me present to you the future Marchioness of Capel . . . as lovely and enchanting a one as we have ever had in the family!"

Lady Fanny embraced Harriet with every sign of approval, and kissed her affectionately on both cheeks in the French manner. She declared she could not be more delighted.

"I don't know what it is about you, my dear," she confessed, "but there is something which it is almost impossible to set aside. Perhaps it is the way your father brought you up: to be so heedless of convention, and so completely unafraid, that you will take the most outrageous risks if you feel it will bring about a desired result. However, when you are married to Richard I hope you will become a little more conventional. Richard will need a highly conventional wife, and perhaps a very – patient one?" glancing at her brother. "We have all had to be a little patient with Richard since the days when he was a somewhat turbulent small boy."

"I intend to become a model husband," Richard assured his sister with curious fervour. "Harriet deserves no less."

"And you have explained to her that we are leaving for Capel immediately?" She turned to Harriet and touched her cheek lightly. "My father is awaiting us there, and the chapel is the very place for a wedding. Indeed, Capel is altogether a delightful house, and I am very certain you will love it. My maid has packed all your things, and once you are married and return to town you can do as much shopping as you please. I shall recommend you to all the best dressmakers and milliners, and there is no reason why you should not become the talk of London in no time at all. With your colouring, and that certain air you have, and your enchanting figure – so childlike and yet not in the least childlike, if you follow me –"

But Harriet had the feeling that she was being unexpectedly rushed along by a whirlwind, and it did not seem to her that such indecent haste was necessary. Why, she and the Marquis had scarcely acknowledged to one another that they could not live without each other, and she wanted a little time to delight in her new-found happiness. And a faint mulishness, inherited from her father, caused her to raise some rather diffident objections.

"But I cannot see why there is any need for this haste," she declared. "I mean – what will happen to Verbena?"

"Verbena will remain with me until your honeymoon is over, after which she will naturally be your responsibility – yours and Richard's."

"A ready-made family," Richard remarked a little drily.

"But I shall like that very much," Harriet admitted, and then sought Lord Capel's eyes a trifle anxiously. Her refusal to be stampeded into marriage without so much as a single protest seemed to have wounded him considerably, and she was upset by the hurt look in his eyes. She said hastily: "It is just that I am a little bewildered, and – and it is putting everyone to so much inconvenience – "

"Nonsense." Lady Fanny spoke briskly. "Everything is as good as arranged, and there is no question of anyone being put to the least inconvenience. A wedding in the Wendover family is something we all take pleasure in, and I am going now to inform Bruce that he can offer you his congratulations – he is waiting in the conservatory to hear that everything is settled satisfactorily – and once you have returned from your wedding-journey I shall suggest that he accompanies me to Italy, which will provide him with some diversion at least. And amongst other things I must see Pauncefoot and get him to lay on a light luncheon for us, and after that we really must leave without any further delay."

She glanced at the two who were causing her so much excitement, blew a kiss to them both and left the room. Lord Capel approached his prospective bride and looked at her accusingly.

"You do not wish to marry me so soon?"

"I did not say so."

"But you are not happy about Fanny's arrangements? You think it is all too – too rushed, and not at all to your liking?"

"Of *course* not!" Very gently she laid a hand on his sleeve, and when he seized it and kissed it she lifted her other hand and lightly touched his cheek. With her heart thundering away beneath her demure robe and her green eyes alight, she confessed: "I have no objection at all to your marrying me whenever you wish, my lord – *whenever you wish*, do you understand that?"

"I do," he answered huskily. "Only say 'whenever you wish, Richard'."

Softly she obeyed him.

"Whenever you wish, Richard."

He caught her to him, and she found herself submitting to some rather violent love making which she found highly satisfactory. It was only when they thought they heard Lady Fanny returning that she managed, rather hurriedly, to ask him a question which she had been longing to ask for some time.

"How was it that you ever became guardian to the de Courcey children?" she wanted to know. "You knew so little about them when I first met you, and I cannot believe that you entered into the arrangement willingly."

"I didn't," he replied. "I met Sir Willoughby one night when he had been gambling heavily at White's, and he was depressed. He talked to me about his family and how concerned he was lest he should die and leave them to the care of no one in particular, the thought of which plainly perturbed him very much. So with no other intention than the wish to cheer him I said I would keep an eye on them myself if anything should happen to him. And the next thing I knew was that he had appointed me their guardian, and I didn't know that until he was dead. The pleasing intelligence was conveyed to me through my solicitors, who seemed to think I had taken leave of my senses."

"I see," Harriet said thoughtfully. It occurred to her that she and this man who was to become her husband would never have met but for that night at White's, and an anxious baronet's very natural concern for his family.

The same thought obviously occurred to the Marquis.

"So far as I am concerned I couldn't wish it otherwise," he said. "But for Sir Willoughby I wouldn't have met you, and if I hadn't met you I wouldn't be the happiest man in England today!"

She smiled up at him.

"With a ready-made family," she reminded him. "But they're such a very nice family, Richard, and Verbena already admires you tremendously. You will grow fond of her in time, won't you?"

"I have no doubt of it," he answered. "But I trust you will not blame me if I spare a little fondness for the members of my own family when they arrive!"

The entry of Lady Fanny prevented Harriet becoming involved in a rather personal form of argument, and it also spared her, as she was aware, a few blushes.

**Millions of women
love Harlequin Romances**

**Millions of women
trust Harlequin Romances**

NOW
**Millions of women
can find that same love,
that same trust, in the**

NEW
HARLEQUIN
HISTORICALS

HARLEQUIN HISTORICALS bring you all the romance
and suspense, all the intrigue and mystery,
the excitement and adventure of an age long past.

HARLEQUIN HISTORICALS have the deep love and
sentiment you look for in Harlequin Romances.
They are about people you will care about. They
bring you other worlds and other times—all against
a background of pure romance.

Historical romances with the Harlequin magic

It was a time of lavish costume-balls . . .
of masked ladies in delicate folds of lace
and dashing cavaliers in pearl-trimmed satin . . .
starry-eyed lovers cruelly kept apart
by the rigid rules of the nobility . . .
secret meetings in hidden, leafy bowers . . .
and the quiet, serene beauty
of everlasting love.

It was the age of romance.

Harlequin now brings you the age of romance

It was a time of wicked conspiracies and dastardly plots . . . of virtuous ladies abducted by the all-powerful lords of the nobility . . . vicious highwaymen and scheming villains . . .

It was an age of threatening intrigue and swashbuckling derring-do, when strength and swordplay were all that counted, and right and wrong were as nothing.

But, it was also a time of pure romance.